Dead Karma

A Swanson Herbinko Mystery

Tulum

Bathsheba Monk

Blue Heron Book Works

Allentown

ISBN: 0996817735
ISBN-13:978-0-9968177-3-8
Cover Design by Angie Zambrano
Stylist Rose Ellen Moore of RC Moore for the Unique Individual
Cover Photo by Paul Heller
Cover model Angela DeAngelo

Blue Heron Book Works, LLC
Allentown, PA 18104

www.blueheronbookworks.com

bathshebamonk.com

DEDICATION

This book is for all the wonderful yogis and yoginis I have known whose knowledge and passion transformed me—Baron Baptiste in Boston, Karen Misencek Carter in D.C., Cat Cappel and Leah Naylor of West End Yoga in Pennsylvania, Fanny Barry of Tribal in Tulum and especially John DeMinico: you never forget your first. Namaste.

Table of Contents

ACKNOWLEDGMENTS

I would like to thank Paul Heller for his editorial guidance, knowledge of Spanish and just being a great person to work with. Also, I would like to acknowledge Fanny Barry of Tribal in Tulum for showing me her beloved city and showing me that it's possible to live without 24/7 electricity and maybe be a little happier for it.

Chapter 1

Downwardly Dog

So, another lover—Guy de Guy—died at the hands of a homicidal maniac, a French one this time who just *happened* to be his sister who was aiming at me. Guy slipped from my arms just as he was kissing me. It's been two months, and I haven't cried. I'm still numb and not from medication, which I refuse to take because it might make me deaf to the message the universe has been sending me which is *this*: I am totally jinxed in love and for the safety of every man out there who finds me attractive I am taking myself off the market. From now on, I am living chaste and pure, concentrating on work and getting myself in shape.

"You can't take yourself off the market," Dick chides me. "You're in your prime child-bearing years."

"Who do you work for?" I ask him, "Me or my uncles?" My Uncles Stevie and Joe are always harping that time is running out to make more Herbinkos. But hello! I'm only thirty. And I don't see them doing their part either.

"And what kind of a politically uncorrect thing is that to say? You think women are just vessels for the procreation of the species?"

"*In*correct," Dick says.

"You think I'm *wrong*?"

"It's *incorrect*. Not *uncorrect*. There is no such word as uncorrect."

"Fine. Whatever."

We join the back of a line snaking up the stairs to a hot yoga studio that Dick has finally persuaded me to visit. "Try a session. Just once. It'll change your life," he's badgered me until I relented. Yesterday I endured the sneers of the shop girls at Lululemon who apparently think yoga is a size-4-fits-all and made them fetch size 12 yoga togs out of the storage room of shame. I cut work early today, dropped Devil Dog at Max's Deli, zoomed down Storrow Drive from Brookline in my Miata and met Dick at the entrance of the Arlington St. hot yoga studio in downtown Boston five minutes ago.

"Did you bring your water?" he asks.

I reach in my bag and hold up the plastic bottle.

"Towel?"

"Don't they have towels here?"

"You can *rent* one," he says, making a face. Dick has a thing about germs.

"I assume they wash the towels between uses."

The people sitting on the steps in front of us suddenly rise in unison as if they're getting instructions from outer space and start to single file into a room at the top of the stairs, just as other people, drenched in sweat and chugging from water bottles or pouring water over their heads stagger out. I try to find the bliss in their faces that Dick is always talking about, but they look so tired they can hardly walk.

"Here we go," Dick says, hoisting his rolled up biodegradable mat, which is secured in some complicated macraméd rope thing, onto his shoulder.

My own mat, a bright yellow one which I bought at Ollies for six dollars, is still in its shrink wrapped plastic. It looked cheery in the store, but garish compared to the ones everyone else is carrying—all muted shades of lavender and gray and brown. I pick at the seam of plastic which is like welded shut, wondering, "What in god's name am I *doing* here!?"

This is the first organized athletic event I have been to since Boston Latin gym where they made us wear royal blue rompers with our names embroidered across the back in white thread. The "nko" in Herbinko was lost under my armpit due to my poor embroidering skills and accounted for the gym teacher calling me "Herbie" which stuck of course till graduation.

When it's our turn at the check-in desk, Dick hands the woman his card which she punches and I pull out my checkbook.

"How much?" I ask.

"Do you have a mat? A towel? Water?" she asks.

"I need a towel," I say.

"Sixteen dollars." She hands me the biggest towel I have ever seen in my life. "Don't forget to drink that bottle before the class and another one afterwards. Do you have one for afterwards?"

I shake my head.

She pulls a liter water bottle from under the counter with the picture of a handsome man on the label. I recognize the man as Hunter Hanna, the celebrity yoga teacher who owns, with his wife Layla, the franchise of fifteen Savas Hanna Hot Yoga studios and who is the founder of the Savas Hanna yoga technique. This studio on Arlington Street is his home studio and Dick says he is teaching tonight. Aren't we lucky.

"Twenty-five dollars."

"Move to the side, Swanson," Dick instructs me as I write out the check and regular clients shove their cards in front of the receptionist to be punched.

"Don't they have a water fountain here?"

"They have to make money somehow," he says.

"*Nine bucks* for water?"

The receptionist scowls at me and when I finish my financial transaction, Dick points me in the direction of the woman's locker room and tells me he'll meet me "on the mat."

I claim an end of a bench, because there is only one enclosed dressing room which is already occupied. Loud sobs come from the dressing room, which no one seems to notice. Dick told me that it's common to cry during yoga class because all your stored up emotions are released when you do the poses. But *before* the class?

The other women in the locker room are all tall and skinny and their yoga tights cling to them like saran wrap. How could I have let Dick talk me into this?

They zoom through their change—Dick says it's important to claim a good space up close to the teacher—and soon I am left alone. I peel off my pantyhose and pull on my new Lululemon tights. All the while this horrible sobbing is coming from the dressing room.

"Hey," I yell, "Are you okay?"

The sobs stop with a sudden snurf.

"Hello?" I knock on the side of the dressing room, because the only thing separating it from the rest of the room is a batik-dyed curtain trimmed with beads.

"I'm okay," a voice whimpers. "I'll be all right."

"You don't sound okay. Are you ill? Can I get you something? Do you want some water?" I ask, although I'd really hate to part with a drop from my nine dollar bottle.

She starts crying again, softly now, and I pull the curtain open a smidge so I can see in. A woman about my age is sitting on a wicker bench completely naked.

"Oh! I'm terribly sorry!"

"Don't be. Come in. I'm sorry. Was I making a terrible racket?" She laughs suddenly. "I always forget I'm not the only person in the room when I'm sad. I'm really shy when I feel happy. Hunter says it's reverse narcissism."

I offer her my giant towel. "You want this?"

"No, I've got tights." She reaches into a tote and pulls out what looks like the twin of my Lululemon set except in the preferred size 4. "See? They just felt so suffocating I had to take them off."

"Aren't you going to the class?" I ask her.

"I don't know why I should."

"I don't know why I should either," I say, thinking I found an ally, "Except my friend Dick thinks it will change my life."

She finally looks at me. "It changed mine."

"No kidding. You lose a lot of weight or something?" She looks really skinny. "Or find focus? Dick is always saying I lack focus and that yoga will help."

"Dick sounds like a wise man. Is he your lover?"

"Dick? No!" I almost spit. "He's..." Here's the thing about Dick: I never know if I should say he works for me—because he's the private detective I hire when I'm looking for hidden assets in tangled divorces which is basically all of them—or if I should say he's my friend, although we don't really like each other. He has this superior air that always makes me feel as if I'm *his* subordinate, but he's always there when I need someone. So what do you call that?

"Well, he's giving you good advice. I could have used some good advice a year ago."

"Why? What happened?" I am happily aware that by prolonging this conversation we are missing the beginning of class. Maybe they won't let us in once it starts.

"Hey, look, I don't think we should be late for class," she says, suddenly. "Hunter doesn't like it."

"You know Hunter?" I ask.

She makes a weird noise with her nose. Then she starts pulling on her tights. "Of course I know Hunter. We're *lovers.*"

"I thought," I look at her quizzically. "Isn't *Layla*...."

"Layla? *Ha*! They're married in name only. He's trying to get a divorce so we can get married. But she won't give him one."

Divorce. Now *here* is a subject I know something about. I fish in my pocketbook and give her my card. "I'm the best," I say modestly.

She looks at it and smiles. "A *divorce* lawyer. I'm Christine Sharp. I knew it was karma that you came in the dressing room."

"What's karma?" I ask.

"You're new to yoga aren't you? You're going to find out all about karma. It's kind of like what goes around comes around. Or you reap what you sow. It's different for every person but the same, too."

What she's just said makes me feel dizzy and I step backwards till I feel the bench against my legs and plop down. It's been happening a lot lately. It can be anything—a horn honking, an ad on the side of a bus for concert tickets—anything can trigger it. If I'm driving I have to pull over and compose myself till I stop seeing Guy's tender eyes going blank.

I know *way more* than I want to know about karma.

Christine tucks my card into her tote then smiles at me. "It's nice to meet you, Swanson."

Chapter 2

If You Can't Stand the Heat….

The heat and moisture sock me in the face when we enter the yoga studio. The mats are about two inches apart so it looks like the inhabitants of a giant can of sardines are raising their arms in unison and bowing low. Dick is in the front row, his hands on the floor in front of him, his head is almost on the floor as well. He pretends not to see me between his knees.

"Psst," I say. "Hey, Dick!"

Christine pulls me by my new yoga tank top to the back of the room. "There's more room back here," she says. "Come on."

She snaps open her yoga mat and places it inside the guide lines made of masking tape which, as I say, are two inches apart from the next mat.

"That's Layla," Christine stage whispers, pointing at a beautiful red head whose mat is next to Dick's. She's wearing turquoise tights and a diaphanous turquoise oversized shirt with nothing on underneath except a large tattoo over her left deltoid which I can't make out. "What a bitch. How can she just be right up front like that as if everything was *normal?*"

Christine places her water bottle in front of her and her towel behind her and joins in the forward bend everyone is stuck in.

Feeling kind of hip—I'm in a *hot yoga class*! Who would ever in a million years believe *that?*—I grab at the plastic covering my own yoga mat and because it's so hot the welded plastic seam is pliable and almost melts off by itself. I flatten the plastic and ball it up inside my towel then imitating my yoga mentor I snap open the bright yellow mat which reveals, to my horror, a giant smiley face in the middle of it, with "Have a Namas Day!" written around the edges. My temperature rises a couple degrees and I haven't even moved.

I stand on the smiley face hoping no one will see it and try to imitate the other class members, although they are moving pretty fast. Up go the arms over the head then we bow then we do something like a push-up, then we're all bended like tents with our rear ends up in the air, which should feel relaxing but my arms are trembling. When I look around I see that every woman in front of me sports a tramp stamp rising from the back of her tights.

I feel someone grab me from behind, both hands on my hips.

"Oh!"

"Square your hips," a male voice says, "Don't tilt like that. You'll ruin your knees." It feels like he's lifting me up and the pressure on my wrists lessens. "Love your mat," he says. I look round at him and see he's laughing with his eyes—my favorite kind of laugh in a man—and then he walks back to the front of the class. Where he touched me tingles as if I had been dead and he brought me back to life.

There are four other people, women, walking between the mats, giving instructions and adjusting people's bodies. I look through my arms at Christine.

"That was *Hunter*," she hisses at me. "He *never* adjusts *anyone*. He probably wanted to see who I was with."

I nod and sweat pours into my eyes and down my nose and onto the mat where I am embarrassed to see a puddle forming. Hunter talks us through a couple more up and downs, sun salutations he calls them, and I feel like my liver is cooking.

"How hot is it in here?" I ask Christine. "I'm going to die."

"Just a hundred and five. Go into child's pose if you're overheated."

I look around the room and one person has her knees tucked under her and her head on her mat. I sit back on my feet, close my fists and rest my forehead on them. I feel like I'm going to pass out. How can this possibly be good for you?

"I gotta go," I tell Christine. "I'm feeling sick."

I roll up my mat and gather up my water and towel and back

toward the entrance to the room.

"Call me," I say to Christine.

I start down the stairs without going back for my clothes. I need to breathe real air then I'll go back up and dress. One of the women who was adjusting people is right behind.

"You can't leave," she says.

"I have to leave. I'm going to be ill."

"No one leaves before the end of class."

"But class is an hour and a half," I say.

"You've only been in there twenty minutes. You can't be sick," she insists.

"And yet I am." I pull my rolled up mat close to my chest, shake her hand off my arm, and push on the door. What is she, the hall monitor?

The door is locked.

"I told you," she says. "You can't leave till class is over."

"Don't you have a key?" I ask.

"The door is on a timer. It unlocks when class is over."

Defeated, I follow her back up the stairs, snap my mat open and plop into child's pose.

"What *happened* to you," Christine whispers.

"I thought my liver was cooking."

"You're funny," she says. "Drink some water."

Miraculously, the water does make me feel better, although I still have a long way to go to get into Crow which is basically leaning forward from a squat and putting your knees on your elbows. Believe me, it looks even more bizarre than it sounds. Not that I could get into it.   And when final relaxation—finally, blessedly, and quite belatedly in my opinion—comes I fall promptly asleep. I wake up to Dick nudging my leg with his toe.

"You going to stay here all night, Swanson?" he asks.

"Where's Christine?" I ask, prying my eyes open.

"Who's Christine?"

"Hunter's girlfriend."

Dick laughs. "He has a different one at every studio."

"She thinks they're getting married, once he gets a divorce from Layla."

"That's unlikely to happen. Layla's bankrolls this whole thing. These things barely pay for themselves."

"Even with nine buck bottles of water?" I look behind my mat for my water. Someone took off with it. So much for honor among yoginis.

"Barely a finger in the dike," Dicks says. "Hey, if you liked this, you should come to a yoga retreat in Tulum. Hunter does it four times a year and one's starting in a couple of days. Change of scene. Detox."

"I don't have toxins, Dick. You do."

I rub my eyes and stand up. I have to admit that I feel kind of invigorated. For a couple of minutes I've forgotten about the baggage I'm lugging around, a big improvement over where I was this morning after two hours of fitful sleep followed by four hours of fantasizing about how Guy called me Swan and how much I wished I could tell him that I missed him something awful but I can't. Because he's dead. "You going?"

"I'm thinking about it. We don't have any big cases. Tulum is on the Gulf of Mexico. Turquoise water. White sand. Always warm. It might be a good time for both of us to get away."

He's right of course. Our last big case exposed the love of his life, Clarisse, to be a scoundrel so he's got baggage too. The more I think about it, the more it feels like a good idea and Devil Dog's never been to the beach.

And let's be honest. Hunter Hanna's smiling eyes almost made me faint. Even though I'm off the market—and so is Hunter, he not only has a wife but a girlfriend who is now my client—I can still browse, can't I?

"When do we leave?" I ask.

"Two days."

"Fine. I'll book our flights." I roll up my mat, putting the smiley face to bed before Dick comments on it.

"Oh, and Swanson..."

"What?"

"Have a Namas Day!"

Chapter 3

Déjà Vu All Over Again

The requirements for getting Devil Dog into Mexico are a lot simpler than getting him into France, but maybe it just seems that way because we went through it all before. I take him to Ashley, his vet, to get distemper and rabies boosters. I was hoping to be in and out of the vet's office in 15 minutes, but I forgot about the wounds Devil Dog got in France.

"What *happened* to you, Devil Dog!?" Ashley says, pulling apart the hair on his neck which is just growing in where Hannibal, Michel Meriodoc's crazed-with-grief eagle owl, sunk his talons in and tried to fly away with him. Luckily Devil Dog was too heavy from eating all that French food.

"It's almost healed, I think," I say, although in truth I haven't been as attentive as I should be with putting ointment on his scars and all. "It happened in France."

"And now you want to take him to *Mexico?*"

Ashley and Devil Dog look at me accusingly.

"Don't you want to go, Devil Dog?" I ask. "I thought you *wanted* to go."

He turns his head away.

"Well, I don't want to board him and Max's wife won't let him stay overnight in the deli." I get an inkling of what it would be like to have a child holding me hostage with her whims. At least Devil Dog can't talk, that is, if you don't count body language.

Ashley calls in her assistant who holds Devil Dog while Ashley gives him two shots. "You're feeding him the organic food, aren't you?"

"Oh, yes," I lie.

"Nothing sadder than a Dachshund whose owner doesn't watch his weight for him. You're not doing him any favors with human food." She arches an eyebrow and peers into my soul.

Devil Dog barks.

"Got it covered," I say.

She writes something on her prescription pad and hands it to me. "*Perro Verde*. Green dog. Get this for him in Mexico."

Yeah, that'll happen.

"And be more careful with him," Ashley says as I snap the leash on Devil Dog's collar. "And be more careful with yourself, too. I heard what happened to you in France."

Dick recommended Ashley to me when I got Devil Dog, so I assume they're friends and that he probably blabbed that I get people who care about me killed.

I give her a fake smile. "*Perro Verde*! Thank you so much! See you when we get back."

I wait until Devil Dog and I are outside in the crisp autumn air before I say to him, "You could have acted enthusiastic about Mexico, you little traitor."

There was a lot of traffic on the way over to Ashley's office in Jamaica Plain and now I see why. A parade is forming. "Let's go look," I say to Devil Dog who is pulling me in that direction anyway.

I think it's probably a Halloween Parade, but Halloween was yesterday. Still, everyone seems to be in costume, even if all the costumes are of skeletons dressed in colorful clothing. Roadside vendors are cooking with the exotic spices I associate with Jamaica Plain which has the largest diverse population in Boston and consequently the best ethnic celebrations. "What's going on?" I ask a family of skeletons who are carrying baskets of food and bottled sodas.

"*Dia de Los Muertos*," one of them answers before they join the parade.

Right. Mexican Day of the Dead. I've read about it. The Mexicans visit the graves of their loved ones, bringing them their favorite food and drink and basically have a party in the cemetery.

One of the kid skeletons reaches in her basket, hands me a wrapped tortilla then runs to catch up with her family. "*Muchas Gracias. Feliz dia*," I say, remembering some of the phrases Hildalgo—*another* lover who got caught in the line of fire—taught me. I unwrap it, pull a piece of chicken out from the flour tortilla and, looking guiltily over my shoulder to make sure Ashley isn't looking out of her office window, bend down to feed it to Devil Dog who eagerly laps it up. "You're such a hypocrite," I say.

In the twenty seconds it takes Devil Dog to eat his chicken, the sky has darkened and it feels like the temperature has dropped ten degrees. The atmosphere has changed from festive to eerie.

I pull my coat tightly around me and jump when I see a skeleton at my elbow. "Oh!" I say. "You scared me!"

"Are you scared of death, Swanson?" it asks.

I feel the blood exit my head. "Do I *know* you?" I ask.

"Of course you do. I'm Death."

The bones on his costume are florescent green not black like all the skeletons around us. I try to make out the face under the heavy white makeup. It looks somehow familiar, but not really. "Death?" I ask weakly.

The specter nods.

"You must have me mistaken for someone else. I'm not ready to die."

"Not yet, maybe, but you're no stranger to me, are you?"

I feel like I'm going to faint. Devil Dog growls at the skeleton. "No, you're not a stranger," I whisper.

My last two loves died in my arms, and every divorce case I get involved in turns deadly. I'm kind of surprised he and I haven't had a conversation before.

"How do you know my name?" I ask.

A float filled with waving skeletons passes by and it feels as if I'm going to be crushed by the hundreds of skeletons pushing forward down the street. They all look alike to me, even though some have bows in their hair or are wearing hats or dresses. Their expressions never change. That's what being dead is. You never get to change. The faces of Guy, my French love, and Hidalgo, my Mexican love, superimpose themselves on the faces of the skeletons surging by. They'll never get to change. I'll get older, maybe fall in love someday again, maybe be a mother, but Guy and Hidalgo will forever be beautiful and young and full of love and frozen in the past. And I did that to them. If I hadn't involved them in my life they would still be alive. The crowd of Hidalgos and Guys presses close and I can't breathe.

"Please, no!" I beg.

I want to leave this place crawling with skeletons and ghosts. Why can't I move?

The green skeleton salutes me with its bony arm. "I'll be seeing you in Mexico, Swanson."

"You're going there, too?" I ask weakly.

"Yes, and you'll be seeing me," it answer then blends into the parade of its brethren marching to the cemetery.

Chapter 4

Can You Cancun?

I don't tell Dick about my upsetting encounter with Death at the *Dia de Los Muertos* parade in Jamaica Plain, even though I have three hours to think about it on our flight to Cancun.

"Did you tell your uncles where you're off to?" Dick asks, startling me out of my reverie from the seat in front of me.

"What? Why? Do you expect something to happen?"

"If you're prepared, nothing unexpected happens, Swanson." A typical Dick dig. "But you should always let your nearest and dearest know where you are."

"Right. I'll call them as soon as we land." But I won't. They always can hear it in my voice when something is bothering me and I don't want to upset them, just when their new restaurant is taking off. They called last week to tell me that *"Le Haut Dog"* got five stars and a rave review in the on-line *Girls' Guide to Paris*.

"And drink more water, Swanson. You're going to get dehydrated."

I dutifully sip out of the water bottle. Ever since my aborted escape from the Savas Hanna hot yoga class, I try to be more diligent about drinking water.

"Are you finished reading that?" the man sitting across the aisle asks me, pointing to the *Yoga Journal* magazine Dick foisted on me so I wouldn't be a complete neophyte at the Tulum retreat.

"Absolutely," I say, passing it over to him. I noticed him at the gate before we boarded: carrying a yoga mat rolled up in its batik case over his shoulder, wearing cargo shorts even though the forecast called for snow in Boston. The only sour notes are the kind of clunky

14

black shoes which seem out of character with the rest of his getup. Most men don't realize that shoes are like the exclamation mark of an outfit. Or maybe they're supposed to be ironic. A really cute guy. A buzz cut neutralized by two days of blond beard. Definitely a yoga bum. Always optimistic that the sun will come up in time for a few salutations. I thought I saw him saying something to Dick as we were boarding but that's impossible. Dick is dressed in corporate casual. The similar haircuts have to be accidental. I try to ignore his easy smile, but it's like someone telling you not to think about pink elephants: it becomes all you can think about.

"I recommend the article on mindful snowboarding," I say.

"Really?" He scans the cover looking for the article. "Where? I don't see it."

"I'm kidding."

He gives me such a big grin I almost cry.

Not. Allowed. To. Feel. This. Way. Why am I so easy?

"You going to Savas Hanna in Tulum?" he asks.

"How did you guess?"

"Your companion has all the gear." He motions his head towards Dick. "Your dad?"

I almost spit out the water I haven't swallowed. "No."

"Mentor?"

"No."

"*Boy*friend?" He seems really interested in the answer.

"*No!* He's a…colleague."

"Ah! Some women go for older men. They think they're safe, but they're usually the opposite. I'm Mark Stevens."

I put out my hand. "Swanson Herbinko."

"That's an unusual name."

"I know."

He holds my hand for an unusually long time and although I'm enjoying it immensely—no, *because* I'm enjoying it immensely!—I yank it away.

"They have a bus waiting for us at the airport," he says.

"We're renting a car."

Dick said he wanted to do some exploring without the group, but personally, I think he has a touch of agoraphobia from his time as a tunnel rat in Vietnam and doesn't want to get trapped on a crowded bus. Every seat in Economy is taken, and Dick has been doing yoga breathing exercises since the seat belt sign went on.

"So, see you at the hotel," Mark says.

Suddenly his smiling face vanishes and is replaced by Guy's sardonic grin. I feel the color drain out of my face and put my hands over my eyes.

"Are you okay?" Mark asks.

"It's just motion sickness," I answer between my fingers as the plane banks into its landing run.

"Look," Dick says. "Coral reefs. Some of the best scuba diving and snorkeling in the world. Outside of the Great Barrier Reef, of course."

"Of course."

"I don't know if we'll have time for any scuba diving, though."

"Oh, well."

"Swanson, are you okay?"

"Of course I'm okay. Why wouldn't I be okay?" I kick Devil Dog's carrier which is under the seat in front of me. He whimpers. The tranquilizer isn't wearing off yet and we're landing.

"Well, this week will be good for you," Dick says. "A week of warm water and yoga and healthy eating." He looks critically at the three empty pretzel packs on the pull-down tray in front of me.

"Pretzels are uncommonly healthy," I say although my stomach is killing me. Every time I eat wheat lately my stomach starts to hurt. I would never forgive myself if I had something as trendy as gluten intolerance. It's probably just part of the heebie-jeebies I'm going through.

Ever since I've been to France, I feel like a world traveler and breeze through debarking (no pun intended) with Devil Dog and customs with no problem. I see Christine Sharp and Layla arguing at the baggage claim and sigh. This is going to be a long week.

Mark touches my elbow when he passes me on the way to the bus and I jump. It reminds me of Death touching me like that at the *Dia de Los Muertos* parade. He salutes and I give him a big smile because his face is back.

"See ya at the hacienda!" he says.

"Yeah."

The airport at Cancun is smaller than I would have imagined and we go right up to a small ATM machine to change our dollars into pesos. There is also no line at the Avis counter where we are renting a car.

"You need to take *all* the insurance," the Avis girl tells Dick.

"I already have car insurance as well as supplemental insurance on my Amex card," Dick tells her.

"This is Mexico," she says ominously. "I *encourage* you to get all the insurance. If you get in an accident in Mexico, you may get arrested."

"You get arrested for being in an *accident?*" I say.

"Yes," she nods solemnly. "It's against the law for an American to have a car accident in Mexico."

"Maybe we should," I say to Dick.

"I recommend," she repeats. "*Highly.*"

"No thank you," Dick says, curtly turning to me. "Don't get it, Swanson. It's just a scam. It's how they rip off tourists. Put it on your card, will you? It's a business expense."

"How exactly?"

"We'll discuss our five year plan on the beach."

I give the woman my corporate card and after she runs the paperwork, Dick holds out his hand for the key.

She shakes her head sadly and snaps her fingers to summon a ratty little man who takes the key and leads us into a pot-holed parking lot. The macadam feels like a frying pan under our feet. The little man makes a big deal out of examining the black Chrysler two-door for dents and checking the tires.

"*Es* okay," he says, flashing gold teeth and holding out his hand for a tip.

Dick reluctantly puts a bill in his hand and finally the man gives up the key.

We load up our luggage and release Devil Dog from his carrier and sit while the air conditioner does its business.

"We could have asked for a white car," I say.

The air, I noticed, is much warmer and more humid than Boston, tropical I guess you would say, but it's overcast and ominous, just like it was yesterday in Jamaica Plain. I shake my head to dislodge the vision of death. "Do you know where you're going?" I ask.

"Hunter likes to start retreats at the Mayan ruins."

"Whatever." I feel myself getting anxious—for no discernible reason—at the word ruins.

Dick notices me pulsing my fists and says, "Look, I'll give you your first yoga breathing lesson. It's simple. You put your thumb on one nostril, see like this, and your index finger on the bridge of your nose, see like this?" He alternates nostrils inhaling through one then exhaling through the other. "It'll calm you right down."

"I don't need to be calmed down," I say. "Don't be ridiculous. Just get us there."

Dick puts the car in gear and we lurch around the same quarter mile course three times until Dick finally finds the exit and we're on the highway to Tulum.

Chapter 5

"If You Don't Know Where You're Going, Any Road Will Do"--Lewis Carroll

Nothing but modern huge look-a-like resorts line the beach side of the highway from Cancun to Tulum. Construction workers are building overpasses right over the highway without closing off the lanes underneath.

"Minimal governmental regulation at work," Dick says.

"I didn't know you were political," I say.

"I'm not being political."

"You're implying that you don't like government regulation."

"My point is that danger keeps you focused. Otherwise driving is boring." He points overhead at a cluster of dangling wire cables.

Dick is being contrary because he isn't really sure where he's going. If I call him on it, he'll start on a jag about the Peloponnesian Wars or Dutch tulip farming or something equally obscure and even if I pretend I'm asleep he'll continue his lecture. Dick knows a lot about a lot of things and I don't think he has anyone to tell about them.

"How far is it to Tulum?" I ask.

"We'll be there in a couple of hours, maybe less," he says.

"You *think*," I say. "We should have asked that woman at the car rental place. Then we would know for sure."

"Actually, we wouldn't know. This is Mexico, Swanson. Mexico is a dicey place. You never know what you'll come on around the next curve in the road."

"The road looks pretty straight to me," I say. "And why would you bring me to a dicey place? I've had enough of dicey."

"Swanson, not knowing precisely when you're going to arrive someplace or exactly where you are isn't always a bad thing. It's romantic."

Along the side of the highway, people are selling produce out of the back of old Volkswagen vans and beat up pickup trucks: coconuts, mangos, tomatoes, watermelons. Entire families are sitting on lawn chairs waiting for customers to stop. A hard way to make a living, I think, even though they seem to be enjoying themselves.

"I'm an *attorney*, Dick," I say. "I live and breathe billable hours."

"I hope this week of yoga will cure you of some of that thinking. You can't slot your life into one hour segments."

"If I didn't live and breathe billable hours I wouldn't be able to pay you. Ever think of that?"

"You're not the only person I work for, Swanson."

"Whatever."

"I'm pretty sure this is the road we turn off of," Dick says, downshifting and looking left.

"I thought you knew where you're going."

"I *am* sure. But in Mexico things are not always what they appear to be."

"Things are *always* what they appear to be."

"You'll see," Dick says, turning left. "Whatever you're used to, in Mexico expect the opposite."

Sure enough, we're soon driving right into the Mayan ruins.

"I told you," Dick said.

I turn around to check out Devil Dog in the back seat. He's wide awake and when Dick cuts the engine in a palm canopied dirt parking lot he scratches at the door and barks at me imploringly.

"Let's look around," Dick says. "The bus from the airport can't be far behind us."

"Didn't the Mayans do human sacrifice?" I ask, snapping on Devil Dog's leash and walking him to a palm.

"Relax, Swanson. Let the serene air of the distant past wash over you. They only sacrificed *virgins*. You have nothing to worry about."

"That's not funny. It's creepy. Why are we here? Why is the bus coming here?"

"Hunter always brings his students here before they go to his retreat. To get them in touch with the continuum of time. Lots of ritual occurred here. This is a magical place."

We walk between two fern entangled pillars into what looks like an open air museum exhibit. The place is certainly old. Lots of pitted stone geometric shaped structures that seem to all be stairways into the sky. I couldn't see it yet but I could hear the sea crashing, whispering, roaring. The sky was so blue and the light was so weirdly brilliant it was like the air was transparent. There was no humidity like there'd been in Cancun and on the highway.

"This place faces dead east," Dick says. "The Mayan priests would stand on that stone platform, see the steps, and call on the sun to rise."

"Not very scientific."

"Maybe the Mayans knew something we've forgotten."

It was like this for me. The sound of the sea—not seeing it, just hearing it—was hypnotic and the stillness inside the ancient walls, I'd never felt anything like it. Dick looked blissed out, but somehow for me the place radiated death and my flesh was crawling and Devil Dog was barking the way he always does when we're walking in Copley Square and suddenly he finds a dead pigeon.

Are you okay?" Dick asks. "You're pale. Drink some water. I was only kidding about the virgins. That was the Aztecs. The Mayans would be happy to sacrifice you."

"Very funny."

A micro bus pulls into the parking lot, disgorging Mark Stevens, Layla, Christine Sharp and four other yogins and yoginis from our flight. Mark waves and I feel a little better and I start toward him but tamp down my enthusiasm.

"Christine!" I yell.

She shields her eyes with her hand, squinting to see me. "Hey, girlfriend! How come you weren't on the bus?"

"We decided to drive."

"*Great*, then we have a way to get around at night. That's the best part of these things. I'll be damned!" she says suddenly. "Can that be who I think it is? What's *she* doing here? "

She shields her eyes to better see a petite short haired woman getting out of the back of a black Cadillac Escalade whose door is held open for her by a tall muscled man in a tight white tee whose arms and neck and shaved head are covered with tattoos. He bends to talk to her. She points and he walks to the other side of the Caddy. Christine laughs and waves and heads toward the woman.

"The circus is in town," I turn to say to Dick but he's not next to me anymore. I look around for him and see Layla and Mark wandering ahead of the group. Good, I tell myself. I hope they fall in love—well, after Layla and Hunter get divorced. Good, good, I pinch my arm, all *good*.

The woman Christine recognized brushes past her and catches up with Layla and Mark, separating them. Layla and the woman move behind a parked SUV, but I can see them arguing, Layla finally shaking the woman off and running ahead to the ruins. Tulum is like Southie, I tell myself. Lots of feuds and squabbles. Except…not.

I tug on Devil Dog's leash to get his attention—he's on a sniffing binge at the foot of a pink flowering tree—and he snaps at me before we trail the yoga group. Dick is so far ahead I can't even see him and I struggle to catch up in my new Jimmy Choos, which, while definitely cool, are definitely *not* the thing to wear on a pile of rocky ruins.

I'm teetering along when I feel a hand on my elbow and I jump.

It's Hunter Hanna. "I didn't see you," I say. "Were you on the plane with us?"

"I just drove over from the Playa to meet the group. We always start with a visit to the ruins." He keeps a hand on my elbow and guides me over the uneven path.

"Does this have something to do with yoga?" I ask. There's something about his touch that is—no other way to describe it—electric. "I thought yoga was from India. Didn't the Mayans do human sacrifice? That's not very yoga-like. And didn't their calendar *end* last year. And yet, here we are." I can't stop talking because of the current flowing from his hand into my body.

He lets my arm go.

"No, it's not a yoga place specifically but it's a spiritual place. And spiritual is spiritual I don't care what you name your gods or what you call this thing—soul, spirit, life force—that binds us together. The great Mayan age ended seven hundred years ago. They had a powerful spiritual life that lingers in this place. And there are still Mayans today. The Yucatec is their peninsula. Most of them have lost their way to alcohol and drugs, but not all. The spiritual force is so real here that it peels the pretense off people and we can see each other in the way the universe sees us. Shamans from the desert come here to glimpse into reality. And yes, the Mayans did human sacrifice. That's one of the reasons I start here. Death is part of life. If you don't accept that, you can't be happy."

"I don't get it."

"You will. You're going to leave here more peaceful than you've ever felt. I feel the need in you and I'm going to make sure it happens. Serenity is my business."

He takes my arm again and squeezes it to force me to look at him and the electricity starts again. He smiles and the corners of his eye crinkle up. If I could jump into those eyes everything would be all right.

We're staring at each other—it feels like into each other, although I don't even know what that means—and for a split second he turns into a hawk, his eyes grow fierce and his brow knits tight, and he lets out a terrible screech and I see him flying away with something—no, *somebody*—clutched in his claws, but when I blink and look up there's only a giant white pelican with a fish in its beak circling overhead.

Devil Dog yanks on his leash and barks up at the pelican.

"Are you okay?" Hunter asks me.

Everyone's been asking me that. The truth is I'm not okay but I don't know what's wrong.

"Did you see something?"

"I thought I did, but no, I couldn't have!" My mouth is dry and I struggle to croak out my words. "The rest of the group is over there," I say, pointing to a cliff that plunges a couple of hundred of feet to the sea below, "I think."

"This place makes some people seers," he says. "Maybe you're one." He smiles reassuringly "Let's join the others."

I hobble along—I *definitely* have to get a pair of flip flops. Devil Dog is pulling me as if something urgent is happening. "Slow down, boy," I say, but Devil Dog is tugging so hard on the leash that his front paws are off the ground and he's barking like crazy and what he's barking at is Mark Stevens who is running towards us. Wow, maybe he saw me with Hunter and he's jealous, I think, but he doesn't look jealous. He looks completely freaked out.

When he gets to us, he bends forward, his hands on his knees, catching his breath. "Christine," he finally says.

"What?" Hunter says. *"What?"*

"Christine."

"What happened to Christine?"

"Dead." Mark points to the cliff. "Christine is dead."

The air feels like dead weight on me. Not again, I say to myself. Another friend. Not again. I bury my head in Hunter's shoulder for solace but the energy he's exuding now is the opposite of serene. He pushes me away. His eyes turn fierce and his brow knits and he lets out a furious scream like the scream of the hawk I saw. Except it isn't the screech of a bird of prey.

"*Layla!*"

Chapter 6

Sleight of Hand

The three of us run to the cliff. Mark scrambles down a steep rutted stairway to a flat outcrop halfway to the sea. The other yogins and yoginis are huddled at the back the outcrop away from the edge. I can see Christine's body from where I'm standing. It's face down on a rock. Her arms are floating without control in the breaking waves. Two men with a litter are wading toward her.

Layla is coming up the stairs. She's in a bikini top and shorts. She's let her long red hair down and it floats behind her in the breeze. Her body is spotless except for a tattoo I can't distinguish on her left shoulder. Her face is radiant. Her lips are moving as if she's talking to someone.

Hunter is waiting at the top of the stairs. "What the hell happened," he demands.

Layla starts out of her daze. "She fell."

"What was she doing close to the edge? You know better than to let people get that close."

"I don't babysit your trolls," Layla says.

The path at the stair top is narrow and as she tries to squeeze by him he grabs her from behind. She whirls and gestures with her hands as if to wipe off his touch. I'm frozen in place ten feet above them, wavering in my Jimmy Choos.

"You know better than to put your hands on me in this place," she says. "Lord Kisin was here."

"This is no time for your grad school bullshit, Layla. You know this could ruin us, don't you?"

"And I was just going for a swim," she says and brushes by him.

I'm in her path. She stops facing me so close that our knees are touching. "What's your name," she asks.

"Swanson," I croak.

I stare at the tattoo on her shoulder which I couldn't make out through her diaphanous shirt at the hot yoga studio in Boston. It's a red fierce-eyed hawk with a tiny body in its claws. Looking out from under its feathers is a brutal demonic face.

"Beautiful isn't he, Swanson? He's Ah Cun Can." She puts her hands on my shoulders and runs them lightly down my arms and back up to my shoulders, following her hands with her eyes until she's looking fixedly into mine. Her air of calm is frightening. Hello, someone just died, *hello*.

"Swanson is a good name. Swan. Swans can see. Don't look too closely and you'll be safe. But is being safe what life is about?" she asks. "'What does the Swan say?" She lets go of me and walks away.

Hunter has gone down the steps. I teeter to the top one, sit down and take off my shoes. The polish on my toes is all chipped. Hunter is talking to Mark. They watch the men below struggle to strap Christine's body to the litter as it rocks in the surf. I take a good look at the other people in our group for the first time. Three women, indistinguishable from one another in their ordinary beauty, and one other man who looks like an older Mark—black socks with sandals, tie-dyed tee shirt, camouflage shorts. One person is missing.

"Where's Dick?" I ask Devil Dog who hasn't made a sound although I'm holding his leash so tight his front paws barely touch the ground.

We aren't the only visitors to the ruins, of course. There are people clustered on a promontory above us and swimmers in the water. One of them, a youngish man, holds an end of the litter to keep it from rocking and Christine is finally strapped in place.

The litter men make their way slowly through the waist high surf. Even from this distance, it's obvious Christine's neck is broken because her head is flopping off the end of the litter like a rag doll.

Soon Mexican police have herded the group off the outcropping and up the stairs and are steering us back from the edge of the cliff. They are speaking a mile a minute in Spanish to no one who seems to understand the words, although we all understand that they would like us to go to the parking lot and leave.

I look up at the incongruously blue sky. A white pelican, indifferent to the terrible thing that just happened, dives past us into the sea and comes up with a fish in its beak. It occurs to me again that I am the cause of all this somehow. That I'm not bad luck just for lovers. I'm bad luck for everyone. At the Jamaica Plain *Dia dos los Muertos* celebration, Death said, "I'll be seeing you in Mexico, Swanson, and you'll be seeing me!" Poor Christine! She just had the misfortune to know me. I start to sob. Devil Dog starts to howl.

Suddenly a pair of arms wrap around me. "You okay?" It's Dick.

"I don't think you should know me anymore," I tell him between sobs.

"What are you talking about?" He leads me and Devil Dog away from the rubberneckers watching Christine's body being slid into the back of an ambulance which drives away without using its siren.

"I'm bad luck! Everyone I like even a *little* lands up dead."

"Then I'm very glad you don't like me much, Swanson."

"I didn't mean…"

"Doesn't matter. Come on." He pulls me toward our car. Nobody is the slightest bit interested in us. He opens the passenger door, shoves me and Devil Dog in, gets in the driver's side, starts the car, and drives slowly out of the parking lot.

"Where were you," I whine.

"I was out of sight, at the bottom of the cliff. I was trying to imagine what the Spanish must have seen when they first steered their galleons into the cove and looked up at the painted half naked wild men on the cliff above them. No one could see I was there, but I could see *everything*."

"Everything?"

"*Almost.*"

"Well, for god's sake, Dick, what did you see? Did you see Christine fall?"

"Not exactly."

"Then what *did* you see?"

"She was pushed."

Chapter 7

Death is an Everyday Occurrence

I assume—silly me—that the yoga retreat will be called off since one of the participants is dead, but Dick assures me that it will go on as planned.

"This is Mexico," he says as we drive down the road towards Playa Tulum. "We have to stay around for the investigation anyway. The police have a lot to do. We might as well do some yoga while we wait for them to question us."

"My thoughts *exactly*," I say.

"A group session on the beach will help everyone get over the trauma."

"Right."

"I made us a reservation at a cabana, Casa Linda. It has enough electricity for the evenings—laptops and everything—and enough for a gas stove. The proprietress lights with candles. It's much better than one of the bigger hotels."

"And why is that?" I ask, trying to find the poetry in not enough electricity to use my hairdryer.

"It's more real."

" Please tell me what you saw, Dick. Did you see who pushed Christine?"

"What difference does it make?"

"If I have to do down dogs in a group that includes a murderer, I would like to know who it is so I don't make her mad."

"They don't want to murder *you*, Swanson. At least not yet."

"Very funny."

"It was specific. And I'm afraid it was calculated."

"Well, then obviously it was Layla. She wanted to kill her rival for Hunter. It doesn't seem like rocket science to me."

Dick laughs. "Swanson, sometimes you are so naïve."

"How so?"

"Do you think that Christine was the only rival for Hunter's affections?"

"I know you said he had a girl in every port. Or every hot yoga studio at least. So why did Layla kill just Christine?"

"We don't know who killed Christine but I'm pretty sure whoever did it isn't finished."

I feel suddenly cold. Hello, Death.

We are driving along the beach. Shacks selling tourist stuff—sarongs, bikinis, flip flops, tees, boogie boards—lines the road on both sides. I catch glimpses of faceted turquoise water between the makeshift stands.

"Stop here!" I command and Dick swerves into a sandy parking lot while I jump out to buy a pair of flip flops at a tourist shop. The transaction is so slow—the owner insisting on showing me every pair of flip flops in stock, then asking other people's opinion on my final choice—that I begin to realize that things in Mexico run at their own pace and my Boston impatience isn't going to play well here. The proprietress finally accepts my money and I run back out and we take off again.

"This place is really touristy," I say. "I thought it would be a lot more primitive."

"It's all new," Dick says. "None of these cars were here a year ago. A new element has moved in."

One stand advertises fruit smoothies and maybe I've been hanging around Dick and his ilk too long, but a fruit smoothie sounds marvelous.

"There, Dick, let's stop there!"

We whiz by the stand as well as a really beautiful hotel on the beach side of the road with a fountain in its circular driveway. A gigantic ferocious plumed serpent is spewing water out of its beak. Everything I've seen so far in Mexico seems pissed off.

"Bridget will have something for us."

"Bridget?"

"The proprietress of Casa Linda. We'll be there in five minutes."

The paved road we're driving on turns into a dirt track and the thicket of buildings and vendors thins out until we come to a small restaurant with a wooden fence next to it and chairs and tables on the sand out front. Dick swerves into a four space sandy lot with three spaces taken up by a black Escalade with gold hubcaps.

"This will be just fine," he says.

"You've stayed here before?"

"It got good reviews on Trip Advisor."

Devil Dog is the first to debark—I like saying that, a dog "debarking" get it?—that's me Bathsheba Monk talking. He trots into the jungle to investigate and relieve himself.

Dick yanks on a bell suspended from an iron gate.

"Bridget knows we're coming. I sent her an email."

"Maybe she doesn't want us now that we're party to a murder."

"No one knows if it was a murder. Yet." He yanks on the bell again and suddenly the gate swings open and two mean looking Mexicans burst through it. One of them is a foot taller than the other who is the same tattoo-covered chauffeur I saw at the ruins. The tall man is swathed in enough gold to appease the goddess Kardashian. He squints at us then stops a foot from Dick and stares at him. They lock into who's-going-to-blink-first postures until the little guy pokes Dick in the ribs with the head of an ebony cane carved with faces that are expressionless yet expressive at the same time like a totem pole. Some of the faces have turquoise eyes and teeth. The little guy holds it towards me so I can have a closer look and he grins to show me he's a cornucopia of riches. He has gold teeth with diamonds inset into the top front two. The big guy takes a final drag on a cigarette, flicks the butt on our car and exhales on Dick then he climbs into the Escalade, guns the engine for effect, and they speed off. We eat their dust and my Southie belligerence rears up.

"Why did you let him kick sand in your face, Dick? I wasn't scared."

"You should have been. That was Amador Melendez and his brother in-law Bernardo DeJesus."

"And they are what? Prize fighters?"

"They both had guns, Swanson. And they were high. Seeing Amador here is no surprise but the little one Bernardo is an enforcer for the Zetas, the most feared drug gang in Mexico. This is not good."

Before I have a chance to ask Dick how he's on a first name basis with drug enforcers a slight woman appears at the gate. I blink. She's the woman who was arguing with Layla at the ruins. Up close she looks about thirty. Short auburn hair. Long muscles like a swimmers. Very fit. And very upset.

"Sorry. I meant to leave the gate open for you. I had unexpected visitors," she says, holding out her hand to me. "I'm Bridget. Welcome to Casa Linda."

Chapter 8

Home is Where the Heart Is

We follow Bridget down a flagstone paved courtyard lined with cacti and fronds. On either side of us are tall wooden plank walls, the jungle outside drooping over them and peering between the planks. Things, you can't see them but you hear them, are scurrying around outside of the walls. A yellow dog, its ribs showing, bounds up the path and jumps up and down until Bridget reaches in her pocket, pulls out a treat and tosses it ahead of us.

"That's Goliath," she says. "He's a terrible watch dog because he loves everybody."

Suddenly the fearless Devil Dog tears through a gap in the planks and up to Bridget, and is on his hind legs begging. I call him to stop him from embarrassing himself, but he ignores me.

Bridget gives him a treat and pats his head. "You call him Devil Dog?" she asks. "Is that to keep away evil spirits?"

I had never considered that aspect of his name. "No. He was named after this chocolate cake that comes in a cellophane package. Two to a package. With frosting in between two layers."

Bridget shakes her head.

"How long have you lived in Mexico?" I say and she laughs.

"I came here a year ago, after I got cancer and then my dad died. Everything all at once. It was the only place that I felt good. The sun. The sea. Away from all the bullshit." Her voice sounds soothingly familiar.

"Don't I *know* you?" I ask.

She squints at me. "I'm from Boston."

"No kidding! Me too! Southie, right? I know I've seen you before."

"Me too! I know where! I was on the girl's field hockey team from Saint Marion's. Boston Latin, you were on that team, right?"

"I warmed the bench and cheered a lot."

"I was their best forward. They kicked me off the team for selling pot to your goal keeper." She laughs.

"You keep up with any of the girls?"

"Nah. It was so long ago. I probably wouldn't recognize any of them now."

She runs her hand through her short hair. "I look a little different. A little thinner. A little balder!" she laughs. "It came back in all curly at first, so I cut it off and started again. Tanner, though." She holds out a honey brown arm.

"One of our group got…had an *accident* at the ruins and I guess the police will be investigating. Christine Sharp. She acted like she knew you."

"No. Don't think so."

I want to say: I *saw* you in the parking lot! But I don't.

"Come on, let's get you settled." She picks up one of my bags and Devil Dog heels to her. He likes her. We have to nip this in the bud.

There are three buildings on the property. A red two story in front of us. A smaller white two story with a spiral stairway that looks like a tree house to our right and a large three story that fills up the back of the property with high ceilinged platform floors that are open on all sides like a parking deck.

"You can have the cabana if you want," she says, gesturing at the tree house. "There's only one bedroom, I didn't know if…" She looks from me to Dick.

It takes us a second to realize what she's asking and we both scream "No!" at the same time.

"Okay. Well, Dick didn't give me the particulars. You can have my hacienda. There's two bedrooms and a bath. Hot water in the evening only. We have solar and I'm saving up to get more panels, but for now we have to make do. It's kind of funny when you realize how much stuff we waste."

"Stuff?" I ask.

"Yeah, stuff. Water, electricity, clothes, paper. Everything. The one thing I learned since I moved here is that I don't need a fifth of what I needed in Boston. In fact, it's kind of cool to wait until evening to get hot water. It makes you appreciate it that much more. And it's fun living off the grid. No one knows where you are." She carries my bag up the stairs to a roomy bedroom with large screened in windows and tatami floors, consigning Dick to a smaller windowless one downstairs.

"Well, here you are. There's bottled water in the kitchen. I put some things to drink in the cooler. Smoothies. You and Devil Dog will be happy up here. It's cool at night. Make sure you use the mosquito netting. We're right in the jungle. There's some extra yoga mats in the corner. People from other groups left them here. Feel free to borrow or take them even. I'm glad you came."

"Me too," I begin, uncertain whether I mean it. She's lost the worried look she was wearing when she came to the gate. But she's lying, isn't she, about Christine?

"Southies have to stick together," I say. "We're *Southie* sisters, right?"

"Sure. Why not," she says, laughing.

"So, if you're in trouble or anything…."

"What do you mean?"

"Bridget," I whisper, "I know who those two men were. Dick told me."

She laughs. "You mean Amador and his midget sidekick? I saw the macho performance they put on for you. They can't help themselves. They're Mexican. Amador, the tall one, he's my boyfriend!"

Chapter 9

Likes to Take Long Walks on the Beach

As I'm putting my clothes away in my room, I hear Mark's voice in the courtyard laughing with Bridget about something. I freeze in the middle of lining up my Jimmy Choos under the wicker dresser. What is he doing here? I go the open stairwell and watch Bridget walk him back toward the open three-story. They ascend the switchback stairs to the open top floor, Mark carrying his backpack and suitcase, Bridget balancing a stack of sheets and towels. Everything in Mexico is so open. If privacy is important to you, forget it! Ever since we landed I feel as if I'm seeing everything with x-ray vision and I can tell that Mark is a really good person. I don't trust myself not to fall for him. And now we're neighbors.

Mark looks down at the hacienda and spots me.

"Swanson! I'm so glad you're here."

I wave feebly.

"We're going to have our first yoga session on the beach in an hour. A memorial for Christine. Let's walk over together."

Bridget comes to the edge of the platform and smiles knowingly. It's that obvious, huh?

"Sure."

I slink back into my room and frantically sift through my Lululemon clothes for something particularly becoming—that pink top with the open back. Then stop myself. This is no way for a woman who wants to discourage romance to act.

I pull out the oversized tee shirt I brought to sleep in, the one I got at my uncles' restaurant opening in Paris last month: "Le Haut Dog" in big white felt letters across a pink XXXL tee shirt. It comes down to my knees and I could easily hide a whole other person in it. There would be something wrong with a man who found me attractive in this. I slip it on over a pair of yoga pants, gather my hair in two pony tails, and try to check myself out in my makeup mirror—

no mirrors in authentic land, of course. I sort through the pile of left behinds then pick up my smiley face yoga mat to accessorize my ludicrous outfit. "Let's go," I tell Devil Dog.

Dick is sitting at a rough wooden table on the hacienda's concrete front porch which faces out from an open kitchen drinking something from a green tinted glass. I sit down at the table next to him.

"Want some?" he asks.

"Sure."

He pours me a glassful from a pitcher and sits back in his chair. "Feel it, yet?" he asks.

I take a sip. It's sangria. "Feel what?"

"The forces at work here. The only way to enjoy Mexico is to surrender to them."

"Forces like no electricity until 6 o'clock you mean?"

Dick is dressed in khaki shorts and a button down khaki shirt and he's wearing black socks with rubber sandals that look like he brought them back from Vietnam.

"It's like when we were at the ruins," he says ignoring me, "it was like I was drawn to look up at the cliff just before Christine fell."

"I thought you said she was *pushed*."

"Shhhhhh!" He looks around. "You never heard that."

"Yes, I did, you said…"

"Shhhh!"

I take a drink, disgruntled. "Well, what forces are you talking about exactly?"

"The spirits. They're everywhere. Don't you feel them? It's like they're trying to tell us something."

"That's exactly what Hunter said!" I say, remembering the vision I had of him turning into a hawk carrying…someone….in its talons.

"When did you talk to Hunter?"

"At the ruins, when you zoomed ahead."

Dick leans his chair back on two legs, tapping his fingertips together in a manner I find completely annoying. "How did he know who you were?"

"I *was* in his class with you, remember? He adjusted my hip position."

"He never adjusts anyone," Dick says, tapping his fingers faster.

"That's what Christine said." I wait for Dick to make some sort of pronouncement on this, but when he doesn't I just say, "Can you stop that, please."

"What?"

"That spider on a mirror thing you do."

Dick rights his chair. "I was thinking. Nothing about Christine's death makes any sense."

"I'm thinking all the time, but I don't have to do this." I mimic him.

"I beg to differ, Swanson. You're not thinking all the time *at all*. Not with your head anyway."

"What do you mean by *that*?"

"Most of your decisions come from your emotions, not your head. You're emoting. You only think you're thinking."

"First of all, I don't agree with your assessment. Are you saying that my emotions override my intelligence? And second of all…give me an example."

Just then Mark saunters onto the porch. "Hey, got any more of that?" He pulls a chair out and flips it around, sitting on it backwards. He has a cap on with the brim backwards like a teenager. He looks adorable. He smiles at me, then Dick, and I feel myself melting into my chair.

Dick pours Mark a glass of sangria and says, "I rest my case."

"What do you mean?" Mark asks.

"Private joke," I say.

"Gotcha. Bottoms up!" He raises his glass in a toast. "We probably shouldn't drink before yoga. But it's a memorial service and every memorial service I've ever been to the people were *plastered*." He chugs his sangria and bangs the empty glass on the table. "Hey, I like your tee shirt, Swanson."

"You're kidding, right?"

"No, I like the irony. *Le Haut Dog* is like an inside joke, right? I like the way you think."

Dick, to his credit, controls a snigger.

"Yeah, kind of like a joke. You coming, Dick?"

"Wouldn't miss it," Dick says. "Leave Devil Dog here, Swanson. I don't think they want dogs in a yoga class."

"Yoga is all about *dogs*," I protest. "Up dog! Down dog! Forward dog."

"There's no such thing," Dick says.

"Just thought it up. You'd think they'd love having a real live dog around for inspiration."

I tie Devil Dog's leash to a post and Goliath comes out of nowhere and they sniff each other like mad. At least he has a friend here, I think, worrying a little about whether my curse extends to Devil Dog too.

I catch up to Dick and Mark at the gate.

"And," I overhear Dick say, "If you like her tee shirt, wait till you see her yoga mat. She's a regular philosopher."

Chapter 10

In God We Trust, All Others…Not so Much

The three of us walk down the sand car track to the paved one lane lined on both sides by cars. "It was dirt just a year ago," Dick says.

I know that Dick goes on yoga retreats but I've gotten the message since arrival that this isn't his first time at Tulum Savas Hanna. Everything with Dick is on a needs-to-know basis. But how come I'm always the last one he thinks needs to know? I feel pleasantly buzzed from the sangria and decide to go with the flow instead of interrogating Dick. Which never gets me anywhere anyway.

"A year ago," he says, "no building was taller than two stories." He points up the shore line where the shells for two big hotels are going up. "They don't have the infrastructure to support this money laundering binge."

"What are you talking about?" I ask.

"This is Dodge City, Swanson," Mark says.

"Not good, not good at all. You won't believe who I bumped into this morning," Dick says

I'm about to emerge from my buzz when Mark puts his arm through mine.

"Check it out," he says as we pass a vaulted white canvas tent with a beautiful blond behind a counter stacked with jars of yellow clay. "That's Mayan Mud. We're going to get a massage with it before we leave, what do you say? On me, of course. After they massage it in, they leave it on you—head to foot—till it dries and cakes. It's a skin and spirit revitalizer."

I peer behind the tent and see a clearing of smaller tents with massage tables, one of them occupied by a naked woman on her stomach getting smeared with the yellow clay. "How do you get that stuff off?" I ask, running to catch up.

"They wrap you in a sheet and you walk into the sea and

unwrap," Dick says.

"You mean, you're *naked* then you drop the sheet and..." I gesture to the beachside cafe across the way where a crowd of people are drinking and looking at the water, "You go into the water?"

"You're such a prude," Dick says. "It feels weird the first time. But I tried rinsing off under the shower in there. It took an hour and I was still picking balls of clay out of my hair a week later."

"You went into the water naked?"

"Yes."

"You probably arranged the massage at dawn when the café wasn't open and I'm not a prude. It's just that I can't imagine calmly walking into the water knowing a bunch of people are watching me. I'd pee myself."

"Very attractive."

"All right I'm a prude."

"You're a gorgeous woman, Swanson. I volunteer to be chaperone." Mark says.

We cut through the café and onto the beach. I take off my flipflops. It's kind of magical that the sand is like the perfect temperature even though it was baking all day in the sun. Mark looks up and down the beach for the yogis. "There they are!"

The four members of our Boston group are there plus half a dozen others. Our three women are doing a balancing pose where they are standing in a circle facing each other, one leg raised behind them, touching each other's finger tips. One of them falters, and they collapse, then they get back into formation again.

"The Three Graces," Dick says.

The other man, Mark's clone, is sitting in a full lotus with his eyes closed, thumb and index finger touching.

Hunter and Layla are at the water's edge, holding hands and facing the setting sun. They must sense that everyone is finally present, because they break apart and stare into each other's eyes before they turn to face us. They are backlit and look like two deities that have emerged from the sea.

Everyone forms a circle around them. Silently, Hunter raises his hands in the air, everyone following suit, and joins his hands in front of his chest in prayer position. Then he raises them again and flows into a sun salutation. When we have finished doing warriors on both sides and are standing in mountain position, he says, "We will do some kundalini as the sun sets in honor of Christine who chose to leave her body behind and pursue another journey."

I catch Dick's eye. She *chose* to leave her body?

Mark sees that I've left mine and whispers, "Don't think. Just go with the flow. You'll love how you feel when we're finished."

He takes my hand and I see that I am the last person in a snake.

"Close your eyes, close your eyes," Hunter commands in a soothing voice. "Trust me. Trust each other."

Layla is at the snake's front, and Hunter is moving next to us but not as part of the line. We're moving slowly at first which feels kind of nice and I'm about to close my eyes when suddenly Mark is yanking me forward and we're running down the beach in a yoga version of crack the whip.

"Close your eyes, *close* them," Hunter is saying. He's backpedaled down the line and sees my eyes are wide open.

"What if I step in something? I saw some dogs running on the beach and I didn't see anyone with plastic bags following them."

He laughs. "Then you'll clean it off. It's only the flotsam of the universe. Nothing more. Nothing less. I'll stay with you."

Layla is running in a wavy line which by the time it reaches me I'm being whipped from side to side in wide waves.

The line is undulating in front of me and I see that everyone's eyes including Mark's are shut, except Dick's. The three graces seem to be in a trance. Mark's clone is struggling for breath. Mark's grip on my hand is steadying, and although I see his eyes flickering, they seem mostly closed.

But I just can't bring myself to blindly surrender. What if they lead us into the back of a container truck and we're sold into slavery, or something like that, you know what I mean, it happens.

And who *are* these people anyway? Isn't one of them a murderer, and I'm supposed to close my eyes?

Layla whips us into a circle and we stop. The setting sun has infused the sky with purple and orange.

"Christine is a spirit now," Hunter says. He joins his hands in prayer position. Everyone follows. "Namaste, Christine," he says. "Namaste," everyone but me echoes. Inexplicably I've started to cry because I know, unlike what Hunter says, Christine didn't choose to leave her body. Somebody chose it for her.

Hunter comes over to me. "You're sad about Christine, aren't you?"

I snurf and wipe my eyes and say, "Yes."

"You saw something when she died didn't you?"

I shake my head and see Hunter turning into a hawk, clutching someone in his claws as he arcs into the sky. "No, I didn't. I was talking to you, remember?"

"It's okay. That's what the whip does. It brings up feelings which aren't meant to fester in your bosom." He touches my breast and draws a spiral on it. I want him to stop, but I don't say anything, I just start breathing hard. "That's what this is for. It's to get to our feelings about Christine. Feelings are meant to be shared."

Layla seems oblivious to the pictures her husband is drawing on my breast, but the three graces shoot me dirty looks.

"Come to my cabana and we'll talk about Christine. She was your good friend, wasn't she?"

I nod although it isn't the truth. I don't know what the truth is any more except one truth is this: I don't want Hunter to stop doing this swirly thing on my breast.

Layla has started dancing. Small movements with her hips and waving her arms slowly in front of her. The other women start dancing too. Then the older man, then Mark and even Dick is swaying. Back and forth, back and forth. All this movement is making me sad and what makes me even sadder is that these people were her friends—Christine even thought that Hunter was going to divorce Layla and marry her—and no one but me seems to mind that she's dead.

"Remember," Hunter says as the circle breaks up. "No meat. No alcohol. Honor your body and it will honor you. And I will know if you have meat and alcohol. You can't disguise it. It weighs your body down and keeps you from getting at the truth that is inside you. And if you cannot reach your own truth, it keeps us all down. We are all one person."

The way Hunter talks weaves a web or something and I feel like swooning and giving in to his vision.

It's so dark now that I can hardly see. I look for Dick and Mark to walk back to Bridget's, but instead a hand cups my elbow. I shiver. It's how Death touched me in Jamaica Plain, except this hand is flesh and warm, not bone.

"Come with me," Hunter says. "We are all the same person and

I want to know what this new part of me is."

I must be looking at him with complete bewilderment because he says, "*You!* I'm talking about you. I want to get to know *you*."

"I'm just an average woman," I say, nervously.

"No you're not. I want to know what brought you to yoga. To me."

"Dick thought…"

"He's your friend?"

"I came because he thought it might do me good."

"Is it? Is it doing you good?"

"I don't know." It feels like he's looking into my soul and likes the view.

"Is it doing you good?" he asks again and touches my breast.

"Yes," I whisper.

Chapter 11

Welcome to The Casbah

Hunter and I are alone on the beach. The sun is gone. The stars are out, billions of them.

"Where is everybody?" I ask.

"They went to dinner. They'll join us later."

It seems silly to point out that cracking the whip on the beach has given me quite an appetite, too.

"This way," Hunter says, holding out his hand until I take it.

We walk down the beach, Hunter watching me closely and me looking at the lights in the dining rooms of the hotels that line the beach.

"Just a little way. If you're hungry I'll feed you.

I have worn high heels for so long it's like I can't walk without them. My calf muscles feel tight. "Wait a minute," I say, bending down to massage them.

"Let me," Hunter says. "I was a physical therapist before yoga became my passion."

He crouches and digs his fingers in where I can't reach and it feels so good I pull my leg away. "I'm okay. Let's go." I wish that Devil Dog was with us. He's such a good judge of character. Unlike me who always makes allowances for bad character in a good masseur.

We finally come to a large white bungalow right on the beach. It's unlit. We step up onto a terracotta porch and Hunter turns on a spigot and washes the sand off his feet. "Do the same," he says. I put my feet under the spigot with my flip flops on. "Take them off," he says. "Bare feet only in my house." He leads me into a large room open to the beach and up a staircase to a long porch facing the water. He swings his legs over the porch wall and sits with them dangling over the beach. He holds his hand out for me to follow suit and holding onto it against all acrophobic odds I do, which is difficult because that electricity thing is shooting up my arm and into my brain and, by the smile in his eyes which I can see in the moonlight, I know that *he* knows it. I know where this is going because, like Dick said at the ruins, the Aztecs would have passed on the opportunity to sacrifice me to the sun. I'm about to announce that Dick and Mark must be worried so I should go, but Hunter puts a finger to his lips.

"Listen," he says. "Listen. The waves are whispering a message. I think it's for you."

"I'm afraid of heights," I lie. "When I was a little girl I fell off a wall at the botanical gardens."

Hunter squeezes my hand and gives me a jolt. "I've got you," he says. "You won't fall. Be still. Pay attention. The moon is doing a dance on the waves just for you."

Now I know what you're thinking. For goodness sakes, Swanson, this is a snow job, a first rate one, but still, get a grip! Well, pardon me. In the first place, I bet you wish you were here instead of burrowed under your feather tick watching Jimmy Fallon. And in the second place.... Well, no second place.

So we sit for I don't know how long because when you're as still as we are time stops. And I don't know how we get from here to there but when I come back into time we're in a bedroom off the porch on a water bed and Hunter has kissed me and taken off his shirt and the water bed is rocking because I'm breathing so hard as he tries to negotiate my *Le Haut Dog* shirt over my head and I start to feel seasick and maneuver myself off the bed and stand up. I'm not ready to give in to this new intoxication.

"I'd better get back," I say. "I can't believe Dick and Mark walked off and *left* me. I mean, I came with them. That's just *rude*, don't you think?"

"There's nothing to go back to. Believe me when I tell you nothing urgent happens here. Just oneness." He reaches for my hand. One more jolt and I'm a goner, and to hold him at bay I retreat to the one thing that will break the spell.

"You said we could talk about Christine."

"If you like. Sit," he says pointing to two oversized pillows by a window moonlight is streaming through, and I position myself on one of them just out of the moonlight so I'll be able to see him better than he can see me.

45

He lights a candle and puts it on the floor between us. It's a beautiful room. A sea blue spread covers the bed which is set on the floor. Everything in the room is low and there are windows in all four walls so that the room is more open than closed. It's like being outside and inside at the same time.

When I'm not touching him the electric current is broken and he doesn't have that weird hold on me, and I don't let myself look at him too closely either because he hasn't put his shirt back on and his body is hairless and toned and beautiful.

He retrieves a stick of incense from a drawer by the bed and lights it and it exudes a perfumed scent. He sits down on the pillow next to me. "I don't bite," he says.

"I want to talk about Christine," I whimper feebly.

"In a minute." He stands again, goes out on the porch and down the steps and comes back with a bottle of white wine and two glasses. A serious tactical error is to give your enemy a weapon she can use when she's almost ready to surrender.

"I thought we weren't supposed to drink."

"That's what I tell my yoginis."

"Isn't that a little hypocritical?"

"The person who makes the rules is allowed to break the rules," he says. "So then who exactly *are* you, Swanson Herbinko? And why are you so upset about Christine?"

"Well, Christine told me in Boston that you wanted to divorce Layla so you two could get *married*."

He laughs.

"You think it's funny that the woman you love just...plunged...to her death this afternoon?"

"I barely knew Christine."

"You didn't *love* her?"

"As her guru, of course I loved her.

"So you never told Christine you would divorce Layla?"

"No, I did not."

"But you were lovers, weren't you?"

"Listen, women are always falling in love with me, men too, because what I'm doing makes them fall in love with themselves, but since they're not used to loving themselves they're afraid of falling out of love without me."

"But Christine said..."

46

"What exactly do you do, Swanson?"

"*Do?*"

"I feel like I'm being interrogated. Are you a cop?"

"I'm a lawyer."

"I see. Well, I'll tell you something about Christine and I wouldn't ordinarily say this, because I wouldn't want to hurt the reputation of a paying customer but now that Christine is dead her reputation doesn't really matter."

"Dead people still have reputations," I say.

"But they can't sue you for slander. You can't libel the dead."

"How do you know that?"

"It's my business to know that."

"Christine was bi-polar and she drank too much and she abused controlled substances and she came to yoga to free herself. I tried to help her but she was a very hard case. Actually, I was going to tell her she wasn't welcome at Savas Hanna any more, that this was her last time. Maybe she sensed that and maybe she couldn't handle it and who knows..."

"You're sure she was bi-polar?"

"I wouldn't say that on the record, Miss Attorney."

The lights have gone back on in my head and I stand up to leave and kick over my wine glass.

"Swanson, you're so knotted up inside you can't stand straight. I can make you feel better about yourself and you know it. I'm right, aren't I?" He touches me and the jolt is the worse yet and I'm suddenly overwhelmed with sadness at my own loneliness and I'm thinking what the heck what's the *worst* that can happen when headlights pour into the room. The tide has gone out and the sand has hardened and a car is racing down the beach toward the bungalow. "Leave," he says and guides me down the stairs. "That way," he says, pushing me to the side of the house away from the approaching car.

The car pulls up in front of the bungalow. The driver lets it idle with the headlights on. It's a black Escalade and the two men who were at Casa Linda earlier get out. The little one has a revolver in his belt.

I whimper and put my hand over my mouth. The little guy looks in my direction for a second then pats his gun and walks into the bungalow. Lights go on upstairs. So much for candlelight.

Even though Hunter isn't my favorite person at the moment I wonder why he pushed me away but didn't join me. I mean, if Dick is afraid of these guys, Hunter should be too.

A woman gets out of the back seat of the idling Escalade. It's Layla!

She and what's his name Bridget's boyfriend go silently up the stairs and I can see their long shadows on the sand from the light inside. No one is yelling or getting pistol whipped. They all start to laugh. I sit down in the sand thinking maybe Hunter's telling them about scared pathetic Swanson. Finally the four of them descend, get in the Escalade and drive away.

I stay frozen, I guess for a long time, trying to process what's happening all around me and to me. In Mexico expect the exact opposite, Dick told me, but this is way too *topsy turvy*. My old boyfriend, Hidalgo—the first boyfriend who died defending me—was Mexican. I always told him I wanted to see where he was born and raised so I could understand him better, but he got mad at me when I said that. "I won't take you there," he said. "It no longer has anything to do with me."

Is this why he was so adamant? This craziness where people I'm talking to turn into birds in front of my eyes, people plunge—or are pushed—to their death in a Mayan ruin with spiritual powers, and everyone who seems normal is friends with drug dealers. "I wish you could tell me what's going on, Hidalgo," I say aloud. "This place is so foreign. And I feel death all around me."

The wind picks up, and the sea has begun to roar, and I stand up because my backside is wet from the damp sand. I hear someone calling my name. The voice sounds like Hidalgo's, like he's calling me, yelling "Swanson!" I shake my head because I'm not sure any more what Hidalgo's voice sounds like.

A sudden touch on my left elbow makes me jump and flail my arms out.

"Hey!"

I turn around. Mark is rubbing his nose. "I've been walking up and down the beach calling you. They said you might be here getting a private lesson. Where's Hunter?"

"He left."

"He left you here *alone*?"

"Well, I left first."

"I missed you at dinner. I thought you were right behind us then suddenly you weren't there. There's a café right next to Casa Linda, if you're hungry."

Mark takes my hand and smiles at me. "I was worried, Swanson. I like you."

"I'm really *really* hungry. I like you, too."

Chapter 12

Fear of Heights

Mark leads me onto the sandy car track back towards Casa Linda.

"Wait a second," I say, "I have to put these on." I bend over and slip on my flip flops. Frankly, walking so close to the ground is a discombobulating experience. I have a new appreciation of Devil Dog trotting around on his short legs.

"You okay?" Mark asks.

"Fine, fine. Just fine."

"Let me take that," Mark says, pulling my yoga mat off my shoulder.

"Thanks."

We walk past several hotels with restaurants and I look at Mark expecting him to turn into any one of them, and then we are standing in the empty parking lot in front of Casa Linda's gate. The café next door is lit up and a couple is sitting at the lone table in front. A stray dog is begging at their table—the woman feeding him surreptitiously under the table—and suddenly I miss Devil Dog.

"I have some stuff in my room. I thought it would be more fun to grab a bite up there. It's wonderful on the third floor. It's like being on a space platform in the sky." He looks at me sheepishly.

There is nothing I would like more than to grab a bite in Mark's room, but I am spooked about getting involved with him. "Are you sure?" I ask. "I don't want you to go to any trouble."

"I got a couple of things at the *groceria* down the road. Nothing fancy. Grocery stores here aren't like the States."

"Nothing fancy is my favorite thing," I say.

Mark pushes open the gate and Devil Dog runs up to greet us. After he gets his quota of affection, he assumes his usual dignified posture and walks away as if he doesn't know me and joins Goliath.

"Typical," I say as the dogs trot away.

"You're not scared of heights, are you?"

It's a funny question to ask because I don't think I've ever been above three floors in my entire life and three floors isn't high enough to be scared of, I don't care what kind of a scaredy-cat you are. "I'm totally fine with it," I say.

Mark is wearing an LED light on his head, like a miner's light. He takes it off and gives it to me. "You wear this. I'm pretty good in the dark."

He lets me go first—I do have the light after all—and I make my way past the hacienda which is completely dark. "Do you know where Dick is?" I ask. It seems so unlike him to not be all over me, making sure I'm okay.

"He had to do something in town," Mark says.

"About Christine?" I ask.

"Watch out," he says as I'm about to step into one of Bridget's cacti with needles about five inches long. "Those things sting."

"I think everything here is prickly," I say, jumping back into the path. I adjust the light on my head so I can see the path instead of the plantings, which are exotic and mesmerizing. "Just different, I guess, from what I'm used to. Are you from Boston?" I ask then freeze. A giant reptile which looks like a dragon blocks the path.

"What's the matter?" Mark asks. He nudges me aside and laughs when he sees the dragon. "It's an iguana. They're all over the place down here." He takes a stick and pokes it in the behind and it moves reluctantly across the path, sliding its tongue in and out like it's catching flies. "They won't hurt you intentionally but don't get behind it, it can whip you with its tail and it can really slice. No kidding. My wife never got rid of the scars from when an iguana whipped her years ago."

I feel some of my pleasure in our dinner date shrink away. "Your wife?"

"Former wife. We didn't share the same idea of fun."

"What? She didn't like to play with iguanas?"

"They only bite if they're male and it's mating season."

"When is mating season?" I ask.

"That's the problem. I don't know." He laughs. "I would say the rule of thumb is: if it has teeth it can bite. If it has a sharp tail don't get behind it. Everything in Mexico has a beautiful side and a dangerous side. You've never been to the jungle, have you?"

I don't know why everyone thinks it's such a great thing to travel all over the place. Look at my uncles: leaving a perfectly good place—Boston—and moving to Paris where they do the same thing they did in Southie—make just about the best hot dogs on the planet—but now they have to do it while speaking French. "It's kind of humid here, don't you think?" I say critically.

"Lots of bugs, too."

He leaves me with the image of jungle bugs dancing in my head and forges ahead of me on the trail, stopping when we get to the building. "If you have to use the bathroom, go up there," he points to some steep steps on the side of the building.

"*Gracias*," I say.

"Then come down and go up these stairs," he says, pointing to the other side of the structure.

I don't know who designed this building, but the stairs are really steep. I pause half-way up and I have a straight line of sight right into the back yard of the café next door. I turn off my head light and let my eyes adjust to the darkness. I can see five people—three men and two women—sitting around a candle-lit table playing cards. A green bottle is in the middle of the table and the men methodically grab the bottle and pour whatever is in it into their glasses, down it, play a hand of cards and start over. The women don't seem to be playing, swinging their crossed legs impatiently. They are arguing about something, but the wind has picked up, rustling the palm fronds and I can't hear what they are saying. My foot hits something—a glass— which someone has left on the step and it tumbles down the stairs, the shattering sound alerting one of the men around the table who stands up, looking in my direction. It's the little macho assassin. He reaches in his belt for his gun and points it my direction.

"*Quien esta?*" he shouts.

"It's only me," I say, nervously. "I'm a guest at Casa Linda. I'm going to the bathroom. I'm just here to do yoga."

One of the other men at the table stands up and says, "*Swanson? Is that you?*"

It's Hunter!

"Hunter! I'm so glad it's you. I'm staying here and…"

One of the women laughs. It's Layla. She says something to the men in Spanish and the whole table laughs. Mr. Little puts his gun away and goes back to playing cards. The other woman gets up and comes closer to the fence. It's Bridget.

"Why don't you use the bathroom in the aerie?" she asks.

"I will." Why didn't Mark tell me there was a bathroom on his floor? Everything is so confused here. "Sorry. I didn't mean to startle everyone."

I can feel Death standing behind my left shoulder breathing on my neck. If Hunter hadn't been there, that man might have shot me. It occurs to me that I am all alone in the jungle and if I had been shot, how long before Uncle Joe and Uncle Stevie would even think to *call*? What good would it do anyway? My cell phone battery is dead and we have about 5 seconds of electricity in the evening which goes to things like hot water and the stove.

I climb the rest of the way up to the bathroom, locking the door—needlessly probably—behind me. A huge glass dish is the sink basin and a sign on the mirror says, "Please throw some dirt in the toilet when you are finished" with an arrow that points to an urn full of dirt with a cup on top which is pushed against the wall. It's a compost toilet. I adjust the LED headlight and look down. It's deep. There's a candle and some matches on a shelf next to a small stack of towels. I turn off the headlight and light the candle, wash my face with the perfumed soap Bridget put out, rub my face raw with the coarse linen towel and look at my reflection. The one positive about not eating is that my cheekbones are sticking out, giving me a slightly chic look. I don't really look like myself. I turn my head from side to side when a big wind blows through the thatch room and blows out the candle. In the darkness I can make out only the vague outlines of my face and it doesn't look like me, it looks like…Christine! I gasp.

"Christine!"

The wind has really picked up and I imagine that I can actually hear her voice in the wind. "Christine? Is that *you*? I can't understand you!"

It sounds like she's crying. What is she trying to tell me?

"I'm sorry, Christine! I don't know who pushed you, but Dick will find them. He's out there looking for them now," I say, which I really *really* hope is true. Where is he?

I start to cry. It's so unfair that no one has cried for Christine. Maybe she was a little crazy to imagine that Hunter was in love with her, but does that mean she had to die? And why weren't the police swarming all over our group asking questions? Doesn't anybody in this country care that someone was *murdered?*

I cry and cry and cry and when I look back into the mirror, my eyes have adjusted to the darkness enough that I see myself looking back, not Christine. The wind is howling and I stop crying abruptly when I hear something scratching at the door. It's an insistent scratch. I hold my breath. Then I hear a familiar whine. I unlatch the door to let Devil Dog in. I pick him up and hold him tight. "I don't know why we came here," I say into his furry neck. I'm starting to get suspicious of Mark, too. Why did he send me up this way? What's he hiding?

Devil Dog struggles to get out of my grasp and runs out the door. But heavy footsteps are coming up the stairs and I cower under the sink until the door is pushed in and Mark is standing there saying, "Swanson, I thought you fell in!" He chortles at his joke. "What are you doing under the sink? It's pouring rain out here. Come on out of there."

I stay crouched under the sink, looking at Mark's feet and wondering why such an otherwise cool guy wears such clunky black shoes. But if we always judged people on what they wore, none of us would have any friends would we? And mostly because there doesn't seem to be any choice, I put out hand and allow him to yank me onto my feet.

"Where's this dinner you keep talking about?" I ask.

Chapter 13

Getting to Know All About You…

Devil Dog reappears and allows Mark to pick him up. We linger before heading out because it's pouring rain.

"Just a tropical downpour," he informs me. "Just water."

"I know what rain is," I say. I look next door, but the group has deserted the table taking the bottle with them. The lights in the café mean that's probably where they migrated. Who would believe me if I told them the little guy pulled a gun on me because I dropped a glass? I definitely needed some yoga to calm my jitters, and I laugh at the thought of *me* even *thinking* that.

"Glad you're feeling more relaxed," Mark says. "Ready?"

And without waiting for an answer, he charges down the stairs holding onto Devil Dog who looks at me over Mark's shoulder as if I am pathetic. I stick my tongue out at him, take my flip flips off—whoever said it was easier to walk in flip flops than heels didn't know what he was talking about—and run down the stairs after them. When we get to the first floor, we duck in and shake ourselves off like, well, like wet dogs.

"That was intense," I say.

"And then, just like that, it's over," Mark says. "That's the tropics! I love the way the rain washes everything away. Come on." He holds out his hand and we walk through the first floor—which seems to be Bridget's painting studio—to the stairs leading to the aerie.

"This is cool," I say.

"It's the coolest place in Tulum," Mark says.

The second floor is a yoga studio. Drop down transparent curtains have bird designs screened onto them. Rolled up mats and blankets are in the corner. Straps hang on hooks in the back.

"Hunter is doing the class here tomorrow morning. We have an Early Bird. You into it?"

"I dunno. How early?"

"Well, to do a proper sun salutation, you have to see the sunrise, so....go figure. You'll be up way before then, though. The chachalakas will wake you."

"What are chachalakas?" I ask.

"You'll know the moment you hear them."

We finally reach the top. The pitched thatched roof makes this floor about 4 feet taller than the others. A double bed in the middle of the floor is covered with mosquito netting. A hammock tied to two wooden beams swings wildly in the wind. "Help me tie the screening down."

We loosen the ties of the black screened netting that rolls down from each side of the room. The effect is that you can see right through it as if it isn't there, but it stops the wind and rain from coming in.

"This is wonderful," I say. "Better than walls, really."

"If you live in the jungle, yeah," Mark says. "The semi-permeable walls keep the house from getting blown over in a hurricane. Kerplunk!" He makes a motion with his hands like a house toppling. "Not so good, though, if you live in Southie."

"You live in *Southie*?" I ask. I don't remember him from growing up and Southie is like the smallest of small towns. Everyone knows *everyone*.

"I moved there because of my wife. And I just stayed."

The wife.

"And who is that?" I ask primly. I try to gracefully put my butt into the hammock but it keeps swinging out from under me.

"That's a double hammock," Mark says.

"What do you mean?" I jump in but it rolls over and I fall out, landing right on my keister. Devil Dog looks at me with disgust, but Mark is laughing.

"That's what I love about you," Mark says helping me up. "You are so natural."

I shake myself off.

"It's for two," he holds out his hand again—thinking to drag me into it with him—but I ignore it.

"You said something about dinner?"

"Oh, right. You must be starving!"

I'm so hungry I'm about to gnaw my arm off.

He pulls out a little cooler from under the bed, snaps open a yoga blanket that he filched from Bridget's studio onto the floor and assembles a dinner. A bottle of wine appears along with two glasses and he adroitly manipulates the corkscrew and opens the bottle. "Madam," he says, offering his arm and helping me onto the floor.

I am suddenly conscious of the ridiculous outfit I put on before going to yoga class, for specifically this reason: so I wouldn't be at all attractive to Mark. So Mark wouldn't fall for me and end up dead like everyone else who ever loved me. I pull my pigtails a little tighter in case they were looking sexily disheveled, and fluff up my size xxxxxxl pink tee shirt with "Le Haut Dog" written in script across my chest in white felt.

"This is the best thing about yoga," Mark says, pouring me a glass of red wine. "Being able to sit like this."

He's sitting in a classic lotus position which I try to imitate but can't so settle for a half lotus.

"It's surprisingly comfortable," I say. And the wine is surprisingly relaxing. "So what happened to your wife?" I ask. "Are you divorced?"

"No. She died," Mark says matter-of-factly.

I examine the bottom of my glass which is now empty. "I'm sorry."

"Have some of this. It's unbelievable." Mark cuts a piece of goat cheese and puts it on a cracker for me. "And this, too," he cuts a piece of ham for me.

"I thought Hunter says we're not supposed to eat meat and drink alcohol."

"Hunter and Layla drink more booze and eat more meat than any couple I know," he says. "That abstinence stuff is just part of their *schtick.*"

"*Schtick?*"

"Story. Routine. The gospel according to Savas Hanna."

I eat it delicately and drink some more wine which Mark keeps pouring for me.

"I hope you don't mind me saying this, but you don't exactly look like a yogin," I say.

"You don't either," he says.

"Fair enough."

We drink in silence for a while.

"So who was your wife? I probably know her. I was born and raised in Southie."

He pauses for a moment. "Regan Stevens. Well, her maiden name is McGonigle. Know her?"

I rack my brain. The name sounds so familiar, but I can't pin it down. "Maybe. Or maybe it's just an Irish name that seems familiar," I say.

He shrugs. "Yeah, maybe. Good old Regan. Of the good old McGonigle family."

"What school did she go to?"

"Mike the Archangel."

"*That's* why I don't know her," I say, "I went to Boston Latin. We were kind of snobby."

"I know," he says. 'I went to Mike the Archangel too. You Boston Latin girls were totally out of our reach."

"Sorry," I say, although in truth I'm a little proud of my one claim to elitism. "How did she die?"

"Do you really want to waste this beautiful night talking about this?"

Devil Dog has settled down with us on the yoga mats. The rain has stopped, but the wind is still blowing, palm branches scratching against the black screens. "Yes. No. I don't know. It seems important."

"It *is* important. I'm surprised Dick didn't tell you."

"I didn't know you even knew Dick. Anyway, Dick never tells me anything unless he thinks there's a reason I have to know it. How long were you married?"

"Not long enough. The more I got to know her the more I loved her. Maybe you know how that is. But I've moved on."

I don't know about anything else he's telling me, but I know *that's* a lie. You don't move on when someone you love dies. You might crawl away from the scene of the crime, but you never actually *move on* until you find someone else to love. "Nice wine," I say. "And thanks for the bite. I should go. Sun salutations at the break of dawn and all that."

He clamps a hand over mine. "Please don't. Was I bumming you out with all that talk about Regan? I'm sorry. She was a great girl.

First love. We weren't together long enough to even get on each other's nerves." He laughs nervously. "It's hard sometimes to know when I'm talking about her too much. Probably *always*."

I nod. I feel the tears welling up for my own lost loves, Hidalgo and Guy de Guy. I always want to talk about them, but I know I am well past the point of boredom with everyone on the subject of them. "Was Regan a yogini?" I ask. "Is that why you're here?"

"Regan?" Mark laughs and I can hear the joy in his voice. He's going to get to talk about her some more. "She was a Southie, like you! How many yoginis you know in Southie?"

"Not too many. Actually, none."

"So why did you get involved in yoga? In Savas Hanna?"

"Hunter and Layla Hanna have other interests besides yoga," he says tersely.

"Oh really? Like what? You know I had to pay *nine bucks* for a bottle of water at their hot yoga studio on Arlington Street!" I start to laugh but stop when I see Mark's face. My mouth goes dry. "What are their other interests, Mark? How did Regan die?"

Even as I ask him, I see Layla getting out of the black Cadillac Escalade at her bungalow and Hunter and Layla and Bridget and Amador and Bernardo the assassin arguing and laughing around a bottle of tequila at the café next door. It was so rotten I must have been totally out to lunch not to smell it. We say it at the same time: "Drugs."

Chapter 14

It's a Jungle Out There

When I stop thinking about Regan McGonigle from Southie as the wife of Mark Stevens and start thinking of her as someone involved in drugs, I remember who she is: her name was in all the papers a year ago after she was killed by drug dealers the night before she was to testify against them.

"How long were you married?" I ask Mark.

"A year."

"I'm so so sorry," I say.

"She knew what she was getting into."

"How so?"

"She was an undercover cop."

That was news the Boston Herald omitted. They painted her as a drug addled misfit, if I remembered correctly, probably to keep her cover. But in the digital age, news gets old quickly and as soon as her story was over, no one dwelled on it anymore. And she's forgotten.

Since I decided to stay, we have polished off most the bottle of red wine and since my capacity is half a glass I am definitely tipsy. "Imagine! marrying a cop," I say. "You must've been always worried."

"Well, you're a lawyer. You think it's less risky to be married to a lawyer?"

"Well, some lawyers." The already black night would get even blacker if I told him about Guy de Guy and Hidalgo. Yes, it was definitely risky to be—if not married to me—involved with me. "I guess no one's safe," I finally manage to say.

"I'm not sure that safe is the goal. If that's your goal, you're never really alive. But you might want to minimize your risk."

It was almost *exactly* what Layla said to me when we met at the ruins minutes after Christine was killed. You can play it safe or you can have a life.

"But you *loved* her," I say, aware of the past tense, and when he clenches his mouth together and doesn't answer I say, "Still do."

"Listen to that," he commands me.

We sit still. The rain has stopped, the wind too, and now all you can hear is the crackling of dry palm leaves. The air feels fresh. "What's that noise?" I ask. It's like something is scratching at the door.

"An iguana." He gets up and lights a couple of candles. "Now we can light these without burning the place down."

The place takes on a rosy glow despite the army of iguanas I imagine single filing up the stairs.

"I wonder where Dick is," I muse aloud.

"He's at the police station in Tulum. About Christine's murder."

My eyes grow big. "*You* think it was murder too?"

"It wouldn't surprise me, I'll put it that way."

"Why not?"

"Mexico is a strange place. Don't you feel it?" he asks me.

"Yes, but I don't know why."

"This whole peninsula is full of ancient spirits…."

"Like the Mayans?"

"Yes, like the Mayans. And their descendants who have never given up their old gods. And there are the shamans in the desert who take drugs to hallucinate and try to conjure up the old reality. And the Catholics who visit the graves of their dead as if they were still here and it was just one big party, us and our dead friends and relatives."

I shiver remembering the Day of the Dead celebration in Jamaica Plain when I took Devil Dog to the vet.

"It's just one big party of ghosts. Not to mention the drug lords who feed on everyone's superstition and fears. They'll plunge the whole Yucatec into darkness if they're not stopped." He punches the floor and I know he's thinking about his dead wife.

"A small fry got her. Trying to secure his position in the organization. He'll end up taking the fall with the rest of them when we find out who was pulling his strings. So what was the point? There's never a point," he says finally. "You can drive yourself crazy thinking there is."

"I lost someone too," I tell him, tentatively.

"Oh yeah?"

Devil Dog crawls up in my lap and I stroke his head while I tell

Mark about Guy de Guy and how he stepped in front of a bullet that was meant for me. Killed him by his sister's greed.

"Greed," Mark exclaims. "That's what killed Regan. The bastards never have enough. They have to get every kid on the street hooked or involved in selling until everything is ruined. Every young life they touch is over before it starts." He punches the floor again. "What did you do?"

"Do?"

"After Guy de Guy was killed?"

I want to say, like he did, that I moved on, but the truth is that, like him, I didn't. I haven't. I haven't allowed myself to even cry, but when I least expect it—in the grocery store getting the wrong change and yelling at the clerk out of all proportion to the tiny transgression, in a yoga class where I am twisting all the juice out of my internal organs—I touch my cheeks and find they are wet and my nose is red and my heart is beating so hard I think it's going to explode out of my chest and I think, "How did this happen? What's the *matter* with me?"

"I helped my uncles get a restaurant going in Paris. It sounds so regular, doesn't it?"

"Actually it sounds kind of cool."

"Kind of cool. Yeah. You know, the truth is, I barely remember anything about it except the opening party, which I organized. And this." I pull out the ends of ridiculous tee shirt with my thumbs. "We gave these away."

"That's some choice swag," Mark says.

I look at him, not sure if he's being sarcastic. "I designed them," I admit. "I must have been in a trance."

"Grief will do that to you," he says. "I painted our bedroom pink after Regan was killed. She loved pink, but I wouldn't let her paint anything that color and so when she....died...well, I needed to do it and now I have this ridiculous pink bedroom and I feel too bad about everything to paint over it."

We look at each other and smile, then laugh, then we are sobbing uncontrollably, hysterically, and unaccountably we are in each other's arms.

He's not gentle with me, but I'm not gentle with him either. It's as if we both need to get out all the pain and anger that we have stored up inside and we feel safe enough with one another to do that.

The wind is howling again and *we're* howling and crying and laughing right along with it. Love making has never felt so *cathartic* to me. The sun is just starting to peek over the top of the jungle when we finally stop and I am almost asleep with Mark's arm over me when I hear a strange sound.

"Chachalaka, chachalaka!"

I sit up. "It's the chakalaka bird!" I cry.

"I told you, you would know what it was when you heard it," Mark says.

We smile at each other and are just about to dive into one another again when we hear heavy footsteps and suddenly Dick appears at the top of the stairs.

"Mark," he says, not even looking at me. "We got a problem. One of the women in the group OD'd a couple of hours ago."

"The one who thought she saw something?" Mark asks, pulling on his cargo pants and ugly shoes. "Karen?"

"That's the one," Dick says.

I feel the chill of death descend on me again and wrap myself in the sheet, all the good karma from the last night redirected from life to death.

Mark's wallet falls out of his pants and it's laying open on the floor and just before I reach for it to hand it back to Mark, he scoops it up and puts it in his pocket quickly. But not before I see the Boston police badge shining on the right side.

Dick has already turned and is going down the stairs and Mark is about to follow him when he says to me, "Go to the sun salutation yoga class as if nothing happened, okay?"

I just stare at him.

"The one that's right down here on the second floor. Probably in ten minutes."

"I remember," I croak.

"You okay? We'll be back soon."

"I'll be okay."

Chapter 15

Here Comes the Sun

I wait until I hear a car start outside the gate before I get out of bed and pull on my clown tee. So, Mark's a cop too. I should have known. No one wears such hideous shoes except undercover cops.

I do a quick stretch and greet the morning on my own. "Chachalaca, chachalaca," I call and the Chachalacas answer.

I notice that there is a small room behind the bed and—remembering that Bridget asked me last night from the café garden why I didn't use the bathroom in Mark's room—I enter. Mounted on the toilet lid is a camera with a telephoto lens snugged through a small hole punched through the wall pointing down at the café next door. No wonder Mark told me to use the downstairs bathroom. No wonder he came clomping downstairs to get me. He must have seen that little weasel pointing his gun at me. Every time I think I've found a friend it turns out that the friend has something they're hiding from me. Is everything in Mexico on a needs-to-know basis?

Devil Dog, who had been asleep at the foot of the bed, is up and together we run down the stairs. On the second level a buzz of yoga students are flipping open their mats and pouring themselves green tea out of a large samovar on a side table. Groups of two and three huddle, looking up suspiciously at me when I clump by. Obviously they heard about the latest casualty in our group.

I run across the flag stones to the hacienda. Bridget is in the kitchen and smiles when I come in.

"It was a beautiful night last night wasn't it?" she says.

I turn red. Could she hear us over the howling wind? Well, so what!

"I liked it," I say.

"Are you going to Sun Salutation?"

"I am."

She pours boiling water into a tea pot. "This is for Hunter. He likes dandelion root tea. Take it to him when you go up, will you?"

"He's not there yet."

"He's always late. So he can make a dramatic entrance."

"Did you hear about Karen?"

"I heard," she says tersely. "Americans think they can take a vacation from who they are at home. This is Mexico. That's not the way it works here. Karen was a party girl and she partied a little too hardy. All these women throw themselves at Hunter and party with him. I don't know how Layla stands it even though it's good for business."

"What about Christine?" I ask.

"What about her?"

"Well, isn't it unusual that two women died on the same yoga retreat?"

"Christine fell. Lots of people saw it. It was an accident."

Karen saw it, too, I want to say, and maybe she didn't see what everyone wanted her to see.

Bridget pulls a bowl from the cupboard and scoops some dog food into it for Devil Dog, who I have neglected it's true. Devil Dog scarfs it up as if he's starving. "Responsibilities don't change just because you're down here," she says pointedly.

"I get it," I say and leave to climb the stairs to my room. Could she be right? Maybe Dick—and Mark, too, let's face it, he has *lots* of agendas here—are seeing ghosts where there are none.

I didn't really notice how pretty my room was yesterday. But it's a lovely shade of yellow in the rising sunlight. Someone has unpacked my clothes and stashed them in a wicker dresser. Probably Bridget. Her thoughtfulness towards me and Devil Dog seems sincere. But her boyfriend is a drug dealer. Say ten times to yourself, Swanson: This is Mexico. This is Mexico. This is Mexico.....

All my yoga togs are in one drawer, all my dressy togs in another, and all my shoes lined up under the dresser. How thoughtful, I think, and grab a Lululemon top from the yoga drawer then let out a scream! A giant tarantula is crawling out from the lining of the bra. I feel like I'm going to faint while still clutching the top between two fingers. Bridget comes running up the stairs.

"What's the matter?"

I point at the tarantula.

"Ugh," she says. "They have nasty bites. They won't kill you, but they will bite. Gimme," she says and shakes it out the window.

"It's like someone *put* it there," I say.

Bridget looks at me as if I have two heads. "Why would someone put a tarantula in your yoga top?"

"To kill me?"

Bridget laughs. "You've been reading too many mystery books."

I want to tell her I've been *in* too many mystery books—and maybe she would like to read Bathsheba Monk's *Dead Silence* which is an account of my adventures in France where Guy de Guy, the love of my life, was shot to death right in my arms, so she can see why I'm a little spooked when bodies start dropping around me.

"It was just so *tucked in*," I say.

"If someone did put it there, which I really doubt, it was just to scare you."

"Well, I'm scared."

"It's a good lesson," Bridget says. "This is the jungle, Swanson. It's beautiful, but it's fierce. Put your clothes on, go to the Sun Salutation and take Hunter his tea like a good girl. You gonna be okay?"

"Yeah, fine. Hey, look after Devil Dog for me when I'm in class, will you?"

"No problem," Bridget says. "He can play with Goliath. They're Southie Friends. Just like us!"

I fake a laugh, grab the tea pot and trudge toward the steps to the yoga class, looking back to make sure Devil Dog is okay. It's just nerves, I tell myself. Devil Dog barks at me as if to say,

"*What is your problem?*"

The front gate is open. A beat-up Volkswagen beetle painted half-assed silver with a pile of thatch tied onto the roof is parked outside. It looks like a car in a hippie days cartoon. Two young blond girls, they look too young to have drivers' licenses, get out clutching yoga mats. They run through the courtyard and catch up to me. Up close I see that their arms, legs, and backs are covered with tattoos, some of them bearing an eerie resemblance to the tattoos on Bridget's boyfriend.

"Are we late?" they ask. "It took us an hour to make it from town."

They run past me and up the steps laughing and I feel envious. Death hasn't paid them a visit yet. If he had, they wouldn't be laughing.

Chapter 16

Nostalgia for the Mud

The class is packed with students—a bunch must have arrived during my tarantula episode—who are already sitting in the lotus position on their mats, eyes closed to the rising sun. I put the tea pot next to the mat facing the students. No sign of Hunter yet.

Karen was part of the troika that Dick called "The Three Graces" and the other two Graces are here.

I snap my yoga mat open next to one of them, not caring how uncool my mat's smiley face looks. I want to yell, "someone has *died* and no one is screaming!" In fact, two people have died. And no one is screaming.

I sit down in a half lotus and try to do one of those alternate nostril breathing things that Dick does to stay calm. I shut my eyes and try to picture what Karen looked like. I open one eye and peruse the students' faces. Of our group the two graces and Mark's clone are here. Of the rest, a few look Mexican but the majority are tall skinny blonds. There seems to be an endless supply of tall skinny blonds in the world.

I sigh and close my eye again and slow my breath. A calm authoritative voice says, "Let's begin. Everyone up, please."

It's Layla. Her red hair is piled high on her head exposing her long neck. She is wearing a turquoise tank top and shorts. The tattoo of the fierce hawk on her shoulder glows red. She snaps her fingers and a man in the front row rises gracefully from his mat and lights incense. She begins the sun salutation sequence and I'm surprised at how deft and commanding a teacher she is. From what Dick had said I thought she was strictly finance.

Layla takes us through a series of five sun salutations. Up down stretch pull up down stretch stand prayer. At the end of half an hour the sun which was gleaming on us has risen above the open wall and in the cool afterglow of its departure Layla puts us in a final relaxation pose and tells us to empty our minds, which for me is pretty hard to do considering that I just made love for the first time in months and found out that not only was my lover married but he was married to an undercover cop who was killed right before she was about to testify against a drug gang, and he is an undercover cop himself and what he's doing in Tulum, Mexico I have no idea, and anyway he went out with Dick to try to find out why Karen overdosed last night and why Christine was pushed off a cliff. So things *naturally* keep intruding on my consciousness and when Layla says, "when an idea enters your mind push it out" I just feel fatigued and as I try to change tiredness into relaxation I hear the chime of temple bells—Layla is walking among us holding them—and everyone is pushing up into a kneeling position then bowing to each other and saying, "Namaste."

Namaste.

"You're with Hunter's group, am I right?"

I'm startled out of my stupor by the Grace next to me. "Yes I am. You are too, aren't you?"

She nods. "It's funny Hunter isn't here, isn't it?"

"I guess. This is my first yoga retreat. Does Hunter do all the practices?"

"That's what we paid for." She looks left and right. "Can you talk?"

"Sure, what about?"

"Shhhhh. Not here. Meet me at the Mayan mud tent."

"Right now?"

"We don't have to be at the next session till noon."

"I'm Swanson Herbinko."

"Julie Griswold."

She quickly rolls up her mat, tucks it under her shoulder and hurries out, turning once to look at me.

I'm the last person to roll up their mat, probably because I have the least practice doing it, and when I finish lining up the edges just right—since when have I become so fastidious?—and look up Layla is staring at me.

"Swan, the beautiful Swan," she says.

When Guy de Guy called me Swan I felt like I was shedding my ugly duckling feathers. From Layla it feels as if someone is punching me in the stomach.

"You've been a busy girl, Swan."

"How do you mean?"

She walks towards me and I see that her eyes are the exact turquoise of the tops she wears. Must be contact lenses, I think, because eyes can't be that brilliant. Up close the underneath of her eyes is a little pouchy, a little tired. Probably from too much partying. She reminds me of what? The only thing that comes to mind is the iguana that crossed my path last night. The brilliance of her eyes is like a bird of prey's. Her fingernails are painted bright red. I think of what Mark said: If a creature has teeth assume it will bite you. If it has a razor sharp tail, don't stand behind it.

"Busy making friends," she says. "Lots of friends. *Close* friends."

"I don't know anyone in the group except Dick."

"Where is Dick? I haven't seen him since yesterday at the ruins. I hope he isn't sick. I hope he didn't drink the water."

"He's not dumb enough to that," I say.

"No, Dick isn't dumb at all, is he?"

I press my yoga mat hard under my arm. What does she want out of me? "I saw him this morning. Maybe he went for a swim. Maybe he's with Hunter."

"Sure. With Hunter. Remember, Swan, what I told you about looking too closely at things. It may be thrilling but it isn't safe. Do you remember, Swan?"

I nod.

"See you at noon, Swan."

"Just call me Swanson," I say. "All my friends do."

She holds me with her eyes like she did at the ruins then releases me and walks away. I do some alternate nostril breaths after she's gone. God, is she scary.

I peer down the stairs to make sure she's left then I run down. I have to get to the Mayan mud tent. Mark said it was a place I *had* to experience so I'm doubly curious. I walk through the yard and pick up Devil Dog on the way out. He seems to have had enough of Casa Linda, too, because he comes with me willingly.

"I might need protection, Devil Dog," I say. "Things are getting creepier and creepier."

He barks assent then he barks good-bye to Goliath who is asleep in a beam of sunlight.

I open the gate, latch it behind me and look down the road. God is it *hot* and it's not even ten o'clock.

"Let's go," I say.

It's interesting to see the sights during daylight. A woman in a tent is selling tie-dyed and batik sarongs and I promise to come back later to get one. Another, bigger, tent is filled with brightly colored Mexican pottery, images of Frieda Kahlo and her paintings on everything from lamp shades to post cards, strings of shell curtains, and an awful lot of taxidermied brown frogs in weird vignettes: four of them sitting around a tiny table playing poker, two in tennis whites holding rackets, one dressed like a paunchy American tourist.

I hurry by until I come to the group of white tents that sell Mayan mud. The beautiful blond Australian woman wearing a white toga flashes me a dazzling smile.

"Today's the day, mate, is it?" she asks.

"It is. Is someone else here? A woman from the yoga retreat?"

"Julie Griswold you mean?"

"Yes, right."

"She reserved two tables together. She's waiting for you in there." She points behind her. "That's one hundred."

"Pesos?"

"Dollars."

I fish the money out of my wallet.

"He has to wait out here." She points to Devil Dog.

"He's a service dog," I lie.

"You don't look blind, matey."

"Well, not a regular service dog. He's an emotional companion. It's a new thing in the United States." Bathsheba Monk apprised me about this new phenomenon. You must have read about it too. Like, people get prescriptions from their psychotherapists saying that they can't function as a total human being without their companion dog so they get to take them on planes and into restaurants etcetera even though they aren't disciplined like real service dogs. They bark at people and other dogs and make a nuisance of themselves but nobody is quite sure whether they're a scam or a necessity in this emotionally needy era.

"The U.S. comes up with the most cockamamie things," the Aussie says. "Whoever heard of such a ridiculous thing?"

"I *know*. We're the avant-garde of this one," I say proudly. I hold the leash up and Devil Dog sits on his hind legs fetchingly, as if he never barked in his life. The truth is, Devil Dog *is* quite snobby and would never bother another dog voluntarily.

"Alright then, mate, but if he causes any trouble at all, you're both out of here."

"Got it!"

"I'm not kidding."

"No, I got it. Really." I look down at Devil Dog who's giving me a there-better-be-something-in-this-for-me look.

She takes my hundred with her thumb and forefinger and it disappears into her toga. She reaches behind the counter and hands me a huge white towel and a white sheet. "Lay on this," she says about the towel, "And wrap yourself in the sheet when you go into the water to wash the clay off."

"Don't you have a shower?"

"Yes, we have a shower. But the tide is much more efficient at getting the clay off."

"I don't know about walking around in front of people nude," I say.

"No one will know who you are. You'll have yellow mud all over your face and hair and body."

"They'll still see me, though, won't they?"

"Who cares?"

"I care." I say resolutely.

"Don't be foolish. You Americans are such prudes. You act as if the world is waiting to see your naked bodies."

She could insult me now that she had my money. "Whatever."

I hold my hand out for the locker key and as Devil Dog and I walk haughtily to the changing room I hear her mutter, "Those Yanks are so stuck on themselves!"

The lockers are wicker and the idea that the lock would actually keep anyone out who wanted in is laughable. Still, I hang my clothes inside, take off my flip flops, wrap the sheet around me and walk back past empty tents—I guess the place fills up in the afternoon with late sleepers—to where Julie Griswold is already face down on a massage table getting thick mustard colored mud rubbed into her hair.

"Not in the hair!" I groan as a greeting.

"It's great for the hair!" Julie says. "Makes it all silky. You're gonna love it."

I tie Devil Dog's leash to a tent pole and lower myself onto the table face up while a Mexican woman adjusts my sheet to cover the parts of my body that haven't been muddied. The two pretty young Mexican masseuses talk to each other in Spanish as they work on us.

When I am finally in position and a cold glop of Mayan Mud lands on my head then gets massaged in, Julie says, "I was so glad to see you this morning. I didn't know who to talk to."

"Are you sure you want to talk here?" I roll my eyes to the masseuses then back to Julie.

"They probably don't speak English."

"A lot of Americans tourists probably do this so I wouldn't be so sure about that," I say.

"I don't care," Julie says.

"So what did you want to talk to me about?"

"You know Karen died last night?"

"I heard."

"You were with that cop last night. You heard it from him, right?"

Did everyone but me know Mark was a cop? And did everyone in Tulum know we spent the night together? Well, we *were* making a lot of noise.

"Did he tell you how Karen died?"

"An overdose. I don't know of what."

"Heroin."

"Is that so hard to believe?" I ask. When she looks at me incredulously, I say, "I didn't *know* her, Julie. I never even spoke *two words* to her."

"Well, she wasn't a heroin addict," Julie says. "I can tell you that. She was a health nut. She never ate *meat*, she never drank not even *wine*. And she would never ever *ever* in a million years do drugs." She turns her face into the massage table. Her body is shaking. She's crying.

Sometimes we think we know someone, but do we really? People are ultimately unknowable. When a friend of mine was in a car accident in high school I tried to give blood for her—mostly because her family asked—but the woman at the blood bank told me that friends and relatives are the least reliable donors. They would never tell someone if they had AIDS or something transferable through blood transfusion. You're better off taking a chance with strangers, she said.

And look at Uncle Joe and Uncle Stevie! They raised me for Pete's sake, but I never in a million years would have thought they'd pick up and move to France, much less open a restaurant there. Sometimes I still think they were replaced by pod people from outer space.

So, was Karen a heroin addict? I wouldn't put money on it, either way.

The masseuse pulls on my hair. "Ouch!" I say.

"Sorry. *Lo siento.*"

She has covered my front and signs for me to roll over and is working the thick muddy paste into my neck and my back. My front and face and hair are already hardening. I feel like I'm part of a clay pot. When I wiggle my scalp, I can feel the clay fissure.

"This stuff hardens up fast," I say.

"So what does the cop think?" Julie asks.

"About what?"

"About whether Karen OD'd. Or if she was murdered."

"He didn't say anything about it. I didn't know he was a cop till this morning."

"You're kidding right? You thought he was into yoga? Why did you think he was here?"

"I dunno. To chill out. Same as everybody."

"For that matter," she says, "Why are *you* here? I never saw you in class in Boston."

"I was there!" I say. "Hot yoga on Arlington Street."

But still, what *was* I doing here? Why did Dick insist I come? It was unlike him to want me around.

The masseuse slaps me on my clay-caked butt. "Feels good, huh?"

"Wonderful," I lie.

She smiles at me as if to say how could you and your friend not realize that we speak good American. She covers me up with my sheet. "A few more minutes," she says. "We'll be back."

The two massage girls leave the tent. Their white tees and pants are caked with mud.

Julie starts crying again. "She was my friend, you know?" she says. "And I don't think that anyone is doing much to find out what really happened. All this weird stuff happens at the ruins and it's like everyone is too scared to find out why. The cops and the media talk about 'ritual killings' as if those ritual makes it okay to murder someone. Like what century are we in?"

"Karen was found at the ruins? What was she doing there?"

"Layla and Hunter do some kind of spirituality mumbo-jumbo at the ruins at night. Karen was all excited about going. The place gave me the creeps. I mean they used to have human sacrifices right on the cliff Christine fell from. Jesus, who would want to go back there after *that*?"

"Did you ever go to one?"

"Once. Last year."

"Anything weird happen?"

"Well, now that you mention it. There was another woman on the retreat. She got into a big fight with Layla. I mean, they were really going at it. It was like a cat fight. I never saw Layla lose her cool. That woman got her ass kicked. Almost went tumbling over the edge."

"You ever see her again? Did she come back to any of the sessions?"

"No way! She stayed until the end of the retreat, but you could feel the tension."

"You remember anything about her? Her name?"

"No. Yeah. Wait a minute. Regan something."

My heart starts to beat fast. "Regan?"

"I don't remember her last name. Hey, anyway. Where are those cop friends of yours? Why aren't they doing anything?"

"Julie, we're in a foreign country. The police over here probably don't enjoy cops from other countries mucking around in their affairs."

So Mark's wife was here just last year. She must have been getting pretty close to something to piss Layla off. And where did it get her? Dead. A day before she was to testify. Whatever she knew died with her.

"What are you, Swanson? Someone said you were a lawyer."

"Yeah. I'm a *divorce* lawyer."

"Well, I don't care what kind of lawyer you are. You gotta help me find out what happened to Karen. And that other girl, too.

Christine."

"Did you know her?" I ask.

"She came to class all the time. Was all over Hunter. Lots of women do that to him. He never says no so he must like it. Look, please help me."

"I came here to learn how to relax."

"You're the only one I can ask. Everyone wants to believe the worst of Karen. And they want to believe that Christine just slipped. Slipped *my eye*."

The masseuses have come back and help our mud stiffened bodies off the tables. They wrap the sheets around us. They push us towards the road, pointing towards the water.

"I'm going to take advantage of the shower option," I tell the masseuse.

She points to the water and shakes her head. She takes my hand, leads me to the shower and turns it on. A tiny trickle comes out of the head. I put my arm under it. It will take about 12 hours for this to wear down the hardened mud just on my forearm.

"Okay!" I say. I grab Devil Dog's leash, wrap the sheet tightly around me and walk with as much dignity as I can to the road where Julie is waiting for me.

"It's just *easier*," she says. "I tried the shower once and I was there all day."

We cross the road and cut through the sandy yard of a hotel past a café that faces the beach. The café tables are full of people drinking coffee and eating breakfast. I groan.

We reach the edge of the water and Julie dramatically drops her sheet, standing there in all her yellow caked clay glory. "Ta da!" she says then she starts crying. "Karen *loved* to do this. She was always talking about Mayan clay and how good it was for cleansing and stuff. She's the one who got me hooked on it. And now she'll never be able to do it again." She wipes her nose with the back of her arm. "She was just so pure."

I wince at her reference to being hooked. Maybe Karen *was* a junkie. What if that's what I find out? That's why it's always better to arrange payment in advance.

I watch Julie walk resolutely into the waves then she sits down dunks her head underwater and starts to rub herself all over.

"The water is magnificent!" she yells. "Look! It comes right off."

She stands up to show me.

I look back to the café. Everyone's looking, of course. So would I. And what does it really matter? I unclip Devil Dog's leash. He can come in if he wants. He runs back and forth at the water's edge, but doesn't go in. He probably can't swim, although now that I think of it, I don't know for sure.

I turn back to the waves and start walking, slowly dropping the sheet, first from one shoulder, then the other. I'm up to my knees in the water and the sheet is dragging but I trudge out and when it gets too heavy I let it drop.

And I dive in.

Chapter 17

All All of Me...Why Not Take All of Me?

I sit down in the surf near Julie, scrubbing the Mayan mud cake off my body, which turns out to be a lot easier than getting the stuff out of my hair. I finally stand up, walk a little further into the water and dive in, staying at the bottom while massaging my head until I feel the stuff soften. Then I come up for air and shake my hair and dive in again, going further out, and repeat the process until all I feel is hair. Silky hair. My hair usually has a straw-like texture because I burn the hell out of it with home coloring. I started dyeing it black in high school because I thought blondes were treated like bubbleheads and my uncles had insisted I start visualizing myself as a lawyer. I'm enjoying running my hands through my hair when I hear my name being shouted from shore.

"Swanson! Get out of there!"

Dick and Mark are waving madly at me. Julie is standing next to them, her wet sheet clinging to her, talking intently to Mark. I look around for my sheet. When I let it drop it must have drifted off. I shield my eyes to spot it and naturally I see a white sheet undulating on the tide.

I wave at Dick and Mark and I yell, "In a minute!"

"Now!" Dick yells back. "Right now!"

I put my hand to my ear and shake my head as if I can't hear him. Then I dive under water and froggie kick towards my runaway sheet. I am almost there when I run out of air. I surface and see Dick pointing frantically out to sea and yelling something that sounds like "Bark!"

"Bark?" I yell back, looking around for Devil Dog.

"No, no, NO!" Dick yells. "Shark! *Shark!*"

Shark!? I start doing the crawl like I learned in summer camp in Maine—you can really book if you do it right—my ears ringing with the sound of Mark's warning that things with sharp teeth are guaranteed to bite if you let them get too close. Faster than a bullet I'm in ankle deep water and I stand to walk the rest of the way in which I start to do when I remember that I'm naked.

"Come on, Swanson," Dick says, matter-of-factly. "We have to leave *right now*." He has Devil Dog, who is barking excitedly, on his leash. "There's no shark. We just wanted to get you back in quickly."

"What?!" I feel myself turning red, head to what's showing.

"We have to get to the ruins while the light's good."

Julie comes out to me and does a buddy system with her sheet and walks me in whispering in my ear. "Find out what happened."

"I'm *not* a cop," I say.

"Well, you're a cop groupie, aren't you?" she says, taking her sheet back and giving me the thumbs-up. "For Karen."

"Swanson, come on," Dick says.

I put my arms out. "No clothes."

"Here." Mark reaches in a beach bag he's carrying and tosses me my yoga pants and top.

"You could have come into the water while I was out deeper," I say as I slip into my stuff wobbling on one leg in the wet sand.

"I liked the view," Mark says.

Chapter 18

Knife to See You

"Where's our car?" I ask looking up and down the road for our rental. The car parked in front of us is the silver Volkswagen beetle with thatch tied on the roof.

This is it. Just for the time being," Mark points to the beetle.

"What happened to our rental?" I ask Dick.

"Blew up." He says nonchalantly.

"What do you mean, 'blew up?'"

"Someone blew it up. Crude work. If they were professionals they would have rigged it to the ignition. Come on, get in."

"And how did you get this thing?"

"Requisitioned it. It shouldn't be on the road. Even in Mexico."

"Which is what you told those girls?"

"Something like that," Mark smiles. "They're nice American girls who want to get into nice American colleges when they get tired of playing around and they didn't want something as silly as a police record on the internet that admissions officers might see."

"Which you told them you would arrange?"

"Yep."

"Did you flash your badge?" I say, letting him know *that* cat is out of the bag.

Devil Dog and I get stashed in the back seat. Mark gets in next to Dick.

"Hold on to the front seat if we stop suddenly," Dick commands as we zoom from zero to twenty.

"Where have you been, Dick? You deserted me ever since we got here."

"I don't think you were lacking for company."

"Who blew our car up? Isn't that something the Mexican police should be involved in?"

"The police are involved," Dick says. "Up to their eyeballs."

"The police blew our car up?"

"They didn't set the explosives, but I guarantee they know who did. This is Mexico."

I groan. The car is in my name—Swanson Herbinko, Esq.—and I remember the woman at the Avis counter telling us to take *all* the insurance because ... this is Mexico. God, I'm sick of that mantra. "So where are we going now?" I ask.

"To the Mayan ruins," Mark says.

"What do you think we're going to find there?"

"It's a funny thing about blood. It's damned hard to wash off." I can see his jaw is set hard. What happened to his wife in Boston had to be linked to the fight she had with Layla on the cliff. This can't be easy for him. But neither of the deaths that have happened since we arrived—Christine's plunge, Karen's OD—involved bloodshed in the literal sense of the word.

We are driving on a different road than the one we came in on: a car track running along the water which is lapping at its edge.

"We're going to be able to get back, aren't we?" I ask.

"Haven't planned that far ahead," Dick says as the car track swerves into the jungle and we bounce past a hand lettered sign that says *Aviso! Camino cerrado!* and I don't need a translator to know what it means. I'm holding Devil Dog on my lap with one hand to keep him from flying out the window and with the other holding onto the back of Mark's seat and soon we are bouncing into the potholed parking lot at the ruins. Dick downshifts, we're going maybe five miles an hour, and he aims us into a palm tree whose base is dented up from similar arrivals. This is Mexico, right? We bounce back off the tree and start to roll backwards. Mark and Dick jump out at the same time. They're holding red chock blocks that must have been stashed under their seats. They race to the back of the beetle and jam them under the back tires and we stop rolling.

Mark starts running down a path towards the cliff. Devil Dog and I climb out of the back seat and stretch.

"Dick, will you please tell me what's going on?"

"When I know for sure, Swanson. I won't speculate. We can't get this one wrong."

"Is this about Regan?" I ask.

Dick gives me his poker face.

"Don't play dumb, Dick. Mark told me all about her. Not everyone operates on a needs-to-know basis."

"*What* exactly did he tell you?"

"He told me Regan was about to testify against some drug bigwig in Boston and was killed the night before she was scheduled to appear in court."

"Anything else you want to tell me?"

"Yeah, Julie, that yogini who was in the water with me? She said she saw Mark's wife get into a cat fight with Layla on the cliff last year."

"Anything else?"

"Isn't that enough?"

"Drugs are a hard business," Dick says. He starts walking towards the cliff Mark has disappeared down. Devil Dog and I trot alongside him. "What do drugs have to with *yoga*, for god's sake?"

"Drugs. Money. Yoga. You can't sustain a yoga empire and a decadent lifestyle on nine dollar bottles of water."

"How much do you know about Layla and Hunter?" I ask. "I mean, are they happily married?"

"No, they're definitely not happily married. Hunter married Layla because she had money. Yoga businesses need a lot of money to survive and she had a lot of it. She's an heiress to a ketchup fortune. But they blew through that before they turned thirty. Hunter's completely impractical so Layla had to find a way to replenish the money supply and she found it here."

"Drugs?"

"Drugs."

"So if she doesn't love Hunter why is she still with him? I mean, if she's the money brains, who needs him?"

"Wrong. Yoga studios are perfect to launder money through. You can keep it a cash business if you stay small enough. No one can prove how many students you have even if you're operating fifteen studios like Savas Hanna does. Selling spirituality isn't quantifiable like selling cars is.

"So, what's gone wrong?"

"The IRS began nosing around."

"Taxes. Of course," I say, thinking of the accordion files at my office stuffed with gas receipts. "But what exactly does Mark's wife have to do with all this?"

"I've been around cops for long time, and most of them go into it with a sense of idealism. They think, "I'm gonna bag a big one, one of those bastards who make life hell for people who have no defenses against them." But if you go after a big one and you don't have backup…well, it takes time to establish your creds, you have to crawl before you run, and you end up out on a cliff alone like Regan McGonigle. Women don't understand power."

I bristle at his probably correct assumption. "So what's with the IRS?"

"Somebody tipped off the IRS that Savas Hanna wasn't declaring all their income and they started doing a full-blown audit. It's never morality that brings down the bad guys. It's the tax accountants. My hunch is that they moved a lot of cash down here and aren't planning to go back any time soon. At least not until the Feds take their pound of flesh. They probably gave power of attorney to handle this to some street smart lawyer. The government isn't that tough."

In a parking space near the entrance to the ruins is a charred smoking mess wrapped in yellow police tape. Inside the tape is what's left of my rental car.

"It happened last night while I was here. They came looking for me but I hid at the same place I was hiding when Christine fell. You should have taken all the insurance on that car, Swanson."

"This comes out of your next paycheck," I say.

"Shhhh!"

We pass the steps to the outcrop that was the scene of yesterday's horror, go up a flight of stone stairs to the overlook where tourists were gawking and taking pictures of Christine's body, and down stairs that take us to a second outcrop at the same height of the first one but invisible from it. We approach the entrance to a large open cave overlooking the sea that you could only know was there if you were standing in front of it. The hairs on the back of my neck stand on end—yes, that actually happens. What a secretive bunch of creeps the Mayans must have been. A police officer wearing a bandoleer full of giant cartridges and a machine pistol in a second cartridge belt at his waist is sitting on a beach chair by the cave entrance. He stands up and blocks our way.

"*Ustedes no pueden pasar,*" he says to Dick.

"*Tengo una propina para usted,*" Dick answers. Unbelievable! He speaks Spanish. He hands the policeman an envelope which he opens. Mark has come down the steps behind us.

"*Cinco minutos,*" the policeman says and goes back to his beach chair.

The four of us, counting Devil Dog, enter the cave. When my eyes adjust I see that there are torch holders on both walls with unlit torches in them that give off a smell like they've been burning recently. The cave has what I can only describe as a natural skylight and the late morning sun has risen high enough to be pouring through it and lighting up the cave like we're outside. "What are we looking for?" I ask.

"I already found what we're looking for," Dick says. "There are traces of blood all over the floor. I think Christine was stabbed here. There's a narrow tunnel leading to the outcrop she fell off. You won't see it unless you know it's there. This is a ritual killing cave. In one door. Out the other. The police claim if someone was killed here it's Mayan business and they can't tamper with ancient tradition or the gods will get pissed. Everyone born here has Mayan DNA."

"If they used to do sacrifices here, it could be anybody's blood."

"Yeah, but that's what labs are for."

"So how are you going to get dried blood off the floor?"

Dick reaches in his pocket and pulls out a Swiss army knife and a bunch of glassine envelopes.

"Christine was teetering around. I saw that. It happens when you just lost the blood supply to your brain. You know, like a chicken with its head cut off running around the barn yard till it keels over."

That was going to be a hard image to get rid of.

"So she did fall off the cliff, like everyone said. But she was basically already dead. Is that what you're saying?"

"That's what I think, yes."

"But why Christine? She was just this naive girl with a crush on a guy who didn't know she existed."

"You're the one who's naïve, Swanson. She was having an affair with Hunter Hanna."

"He told me she was delusional."

"I doubt it. They were hot and heavy. Hunter probably told her he was going to divorce Layla and marry her just to keep her mouth shut. I think that when she realized he wasn't going to do that she thought she would get back at him by siccing the IRS on him. 'Hell hath no fury like a woman scorned.' That's..."

It's so annoying the way Dick thinks I haven't heard of anything that was said before 1984.

"I know who that is, Dick. That's Shakespeare."

"Wrong. William Congreve. People always mistake his best lines for Shakespeare's."

"Whatever. So because she found out that he was cheating by not declaring towel and mat fees, she had to die?"

"No, Swanson. She had to die because she sicced the IRS on the Savas Hannas organization and the real source of their income was in danger of being exposed. That's what I think so far anyway. But the situation here is lot murkier than what we thought we'd find when we got here so I'm not absolutely positive about anything. Yet."

"But why did Karen have to die? You think she was having an affair with Hunter too?"

"Probably. But the question is, what did she know? Did Julie tell you anything about her?"

"Just that there was no way she could have self-administered a heroin overdose because she was pure. Didn't smoke, didn't drink, didn't do drugs, didn't eat meat."

Dick is kneeling on the floor taking scrapings where the blood looks darkest. He's moving quickly because the sun is moving too and the light it's casting is shifting.

"You think Karen was stabbed here too?"

"Maybe. But we can't know unless we get to match these scrapings against their bodies DNA."

"Which won't happen until their families come down to claim their bodies, right?"

"Yeah, they've got both the bodies but won't let anyone see them."

Mark is talking to the guard who is looking over his shoulder into the cave.

"Give him another tip," Dick says, and hands me a twenty. The shifting light is right on Dick. "Tell him I'm praying."

I walk up to the policeman and smile my best smile. "*Buenos dias!*" I say. He auto-touches the brim of his cap. "We're archeologists."

The policeman shakes his head.

"*Arqueólogos*," Mark says.

"You speak enough Spanish to tell him I'm writing a book about the Mayans and want to see the place where their priests stood to call back the sun?"

As Mark does his best to translate what I've said I slip the twenty into the policeman's bandoleer and pat it.

"Okay, *por un minuto*. I point you it, *sí?*"

"*Si, si, excelente*," Mark says. "*Si, si!*" I echo and we start towards the stairs when Devil Dog comes tearing out of the cave yapping.

"Devil Dog, *dear!*" I bend down to pat him but he escapes my grip and runs back into the cave past Dick and starts barking at the wall. He's clearly gone *loco*.

"Devil Dog, come back here you. Just a *momento*," I say and go back into the cave to see what all the barking is about. Dick has gotten up to see what Devil Dog is so excited about. I think he trusts Devil Dog's hunches more than he trusts mine. Dick pats the wall above Devil Dog and all of a sudden a door the size of a wall safe slowly opens.

"Oh my god," Dick says, looking in. "Good *dog*. *Very* good dog."

"What is it?" I crane my neck to see in.

Dick hesitates for a split second like he's afraid Cleopatra's adder might be in there—yes, I read Antony and Cleopatra in college—then he reaches in and brings out a jewel encrusted dagger in a jewel encrusted sheath. He holds it in both hands. The sunlight is on it and the jewels vogue their magnificence. I gasp in amazement.

"Is that?" I ask.

Dick nods and Devil Dog keeps barking, but now it's at the policeman who has come into the cave with his gun drawn.

"You are under arrest," he says in English.

"For *what?*" I ask indignantly. "We're *arqueólogos*. If you let us take this with us I'll dedicate a chapter of my book to you. "

I'm relieved to see that Mark isn't behind him. He must have walked the other way when the policeman came in.

The policeman is pointing his gun at Dick's hands but the sun shifts off the dagger into the policeman's eyes.

You know how when you turn off a bright light your eyes are useless until they adjust? I can't see a thing anymore. Neither can the policeman. "Dick?" I say, putting my arms out to where he was just standing. He's gone.

"*Usted entonce, senorita.* You come with me," the policeman says.

"I'm an *arqueólogo*" I say. "On a grant from Mexico U. I'm very *famosa.* I have the ear of *el presidente.*"

The policeman snaps a pair of handcuffs on my wrists. I give Devil Dog who has been barking at my feet a good kick. I don't think they recycle dogs here. *Le Haut Dog* takes on a new meaning. "*Vamoose,*" I say and kick him again.

And Devil Dog, leash trailing, runs away.

Chapter 19

Déjà vu All Over Again, Again

"I have a right to contact the American consulate," I say as the policeman pushes me into the back seat of his car.

"Please speak Spanish," he says.

"And I have a right to a translator, mister."

He taps a button to start the flashing light and siren and we take off. Me, a hardened criminal. I pray that Devil Dog either goes back to Casa Linda or finds Dick. I close my eyes. "Run, Devil Dog, run," I pray.

We speed along the main road and in half an hour we're in front of a jail that looks like a fortress—not unlike the ruins. A guard with a hefty machine gun waves us through a barbed wire perimeter. My arrester opens the back door and I wiggle out. Everyone's heard about Mexican jails. They're like the Hotel California—you can check in, but you can never check out. And *buenos dias* and a winning smile are as deep as I've dipped into Spanish.

"I won't answer any questions until I have an attorney," I say as he pushes me through a door where an official sits behind a high desk, looking down at me. I hear screaming and yelling coming from somewhere behind him.

The policeman and the official have an animated conversation in Spanish, then the official jerks his head and the policeman tips his cap to me and leaves. My arrester was a known quantity. Now I'm scared.

"I'm allowed to call the American Consulate," I say.

"*Ciertamente.* But that doesn't change the fact that you are an accomplice in the theft of a Mayan artifact you and your gang members undoubtedly intend to smuggle out of the country and sell at Sotheby's." He pauses to let his perfect English and his knowledge of how we Westerners think we can loot the ancient world with impunity sink in. He sees I'm speechless. "Texas A and M," he says. "Go Aggies."

I look around. There is no one here to help me. Pleas for a lawyer or a call to the American consulate—I may as well be talking to myself. I've read about Americans being framed and rotting in Mexican jails, their consulate's intervention notwithstanding.

"I'm just an archeologist," I say weakly.

"I don't think so," Texas A and M says. He presses a button and another policeman appears, puts his arm through mine and leads me away. "Don't I have to be charged with something?"

"You have to prove we *shouldn't* charge you with something. This is Mexico."

The policeman nudges me down a long hall. The screaming and yelling get more immediate. The finality of my situation begins to sink in. I may actually die in a Mexican jail. I may never see my Uncle Joe and Uncle Stevie again. I may never see Dick and Mark again. I may never see Devil Dog again. I swallow hard. I will not let these people see me cry.

"*Senorita*," the cop says as we get to a cell holding five young women, all of whom have young children with them. "*Aqui.*" He opens the cell door, pushes me inside, tips his cap and slams it shut behind me.

I stand there frozen while the women check me out. The smell is overwhelming, as if no one has bathed in weeks.

"*Buenos dias*," I say.

I get a couple of "*Holas*" back.

One of the young women with a kid on her hip comes up to me. "You American?" she asks.

I nod.

"Give me money."

"I don't have money."

She spits on the floor ay my feet. "All Americans have money. My *nina* needs to eat." She holds her kid up to me so I can inspect her. She's about two years old with black braids and is in serious need of a diaper change.

"I wish I could help you but I don't have money on me. I'm not lying."

"Then you're going to starve in here with us," she says.

"Don't they feed you?"

"If you got money, they give you food. It's easy."

She sits down on the floor in the corner, her kid on her lap, glaring at me.

"Is there some water in here?" I ask her.

"If you got money, you can buy water. If no, no water."

"Oh." I am going to last about one hour in here. I start to get angry over the injustice of charging for water, but really, how is this any different from Hunter Hanna's nine dollar bottles of water? The only difference was I was free to leave hot yoga class. No wait, I wasn't. I feel dizzy.

The other women with kids are half asleep probably because they're dehydrated. One of them sits up and says to me ominously. "Americanos are rich. Buy us some water."

"I don't have any money!" I say. "Look!" I turn my yoga pants pockets inside out.

"You got it somewhere," she says, looking at my chest. "Who ever heard of an Americano without money?"

The rest of the women rouse themselves and suddenly the whole place is chattering in Spanish, then shouting in Spanish, then pointing at me accusingly. By their gestures I get the message that they want to search certain parts of me. I am near fainting from the stink.

"Why are you here?" the first woman asks me. "*Drogas?* Selling *drogas?*"

"No."

She gets up, daughter on her hip, and comes close to my face. "Then what? You kill somebody?"

I know when you are in a situation where you are at a disadvantage that the best thing to do is try to figure out the psychology of your opponents. But I am at a loss. Would they back off if I tell them that yes I murdered someone? Or if I tell them the truth—that I am here for allegedly stealing a national treasure— would they beat me up? What if I tell them that their national treasure was probably used to kill two friends of mine? Would that give me creds?

"Why do they let you keep your kids here?" I ask.

"It's not a kindness thing if that's what you are thinking. They starve in here. They starve out there. No one cares."

I want to sit down on the cement floor but it has giant cracks in it full of some kind of fluid—I'd rather not think what kind. The screams of the male inmates down the hall permeate the air in the cell, taking up room until there is nowhere left for anything except the gigantic stench which I am now scared is attaching itself to me.

"Where are your kids?" the woman asks me.

"I don't have kids."

"Are you lesbo?"

"No, I'm not a lesbo. I just haven't met the right man yet. To have kids with." Which I immediately realize must sound like such bullshit to this woman. "What did you do?" I ask her.

"I killed my husband," she says.

"Was he a drug dealer? Did he beat you?"

"Yes, he was a drug dealer. But that's not why I killed him," she says. "He was making good money for me and my *nina.*"

"Then he beat you?"

"Yes, he beat me. All Mexican men beat their women."

"Then…what?"

"He was sleeping with my sister."

"Your *little* sister?" I ask, imagining a child abuse case. This woman was maybe eighteen.

"No, not little. My oldest sister. She's *very* ugly. It was an insult to me. And to him that he would do such a thing to disrespect himself. I told him right before I put the knife into his chest. You are *desgraciado.*"

I feel my rib cage which is decidedly pronounced because I haven't had a decent meal since I landed in Cancun yesterday.

"It's our way," she says. "You take my heart, I take yours."

"If it's your way, why were you arrested?"

"Well," she says indignantly, "It's illegal to *kill* someone, even if they deserve it. This is a civilized country."

"Well, how come you didn't take his money before they arrested you? You must have known you would need it in here."

"My husband's boss. She came and took all the money from the house. She didn't leave any for my baby and me. And she called the police to arrest me."

"Your husband's boss is a *she?*"

The woman looks scared, like she had just made a mistake. She leans and whispers to me with her awful breath. "Yes, a woman. An Americana. But not like you." She gestures at me derisively. "She is big power. A witch I think because she has red hair." She makes a big arc with her arms. "And she wears the tattoo of Au Cun Can on her shoulder and ....." Her face looks suddenly stricken and she stares beyond me and I turn to see what she's staring at because she scurries to a corner and covers her child with her body and there on the other side of the bars is Layla.

Chapter 20

Whatever Layla Wants, Layla Gets

Layla points at me, turns and walks away. The guard opens the cell door, reaches in and yanks me out.

"Hey," I say. "Watch it!"

I catch up with Layla at the check-out counter as she's handing the desk sergeant a folded bill. He comes around from his desk and runs ahead to hold the door to the parking lot open for us.

"I told you not to look too closely, didn't I, Swan? Didn't I say those very words to you?"

"I wasn't looking at anything! I was having a mud massage when…"

"I don't care, Swan. You looked. So now I'll help you. You're welcome."

"That was easy," I say.

"It's easy because of who I am," Layla says. "You need a ride, of course."

We climb into her open yellow Jeep and crawl into downtown Tulum. We sit at an intersection with a broken traffic light while a lone policeman in the middle of the pocked street tries to direct the tangle of angry drivers. Pedestrians weave around the jeep. Several look at Layla intently as if they know who she is, but it's not a happy recognition.

"People seem to know you," I say. " Maybe it's your beautiful hair."

"No, they know who I am. I didn't know myself until I came here. It's funny how you can be one person in one place and another in another place. I think you know what I mean, Swan."

"Like when you go to Las Vegas and you act like a different person than who you are at home?"

For the first time since I've met her Layla laughs. "Kind of like that, yes. When I lived in Marblehead I was just another rich Wasp girl with ginger hair."

She looks at me and I nod. She was just the kind of girl I was intimidated by at Boston Latin. Smart, beautiful, rich and entitled.

"And then I came here for research."

"*Research?*"

"For my doctoral thesis in Anthropology at UMass."

"You have a *doctorate?*"

"I never completed it. A few weeks before I was to leave I went to a tattoo parlor in the Combat Zone. On a lark. With a girlfriend. The tattoo artist read us as a pair of rich bitch airheads and was showing us images that would make us feel daring but were harmless. My girlfriend picked a rose inside a heart for the bottom of her spine. I chose this one." She touches the tattoo of the red hawk with a demon in its feathers and a body in its talons. "My girlfriend said you're kidding at first then she said tattoo it on your butt it will scare your new boyfriend. I had just started dating Hunter."

I was a step behind whatever Layla was trying to tell me so I decided to buy time by babbling. "Wow, all that college ... my uncles would never ... they put me..."

"Pay attention, Swan. I'm telling you this for a reason. When I came here I knew immediately that I was more than a student of the ancient Yucatec. I knew that I was descended from the royal lineage of Maya."

The traffic cop signals that it's our turn and we inch across the intersection.

"I don't understand," I say. "You don't look Mexican. You don't look Mayan either." The people around us were squat and square. Layla was long and graceful.

"Of course I don't look like..." she gestures at the swarm around us "...these. Entirely different. I am descended from the massacred sixteen."

I laugh nervously. "I thought all the original Mayans were wiped out a thousand years ago."

"There were bloody wars of succession between the royals. Too many princes. My family was massacred in the 9th century. Sixteen of us were found in a mass grave. But there were seventeen. It's documented in a cave at the ruins. Seventeen. My blood ancestor got away."

"Layla, how do you know this?"

"She touches her shoulder. "Ah Cun Can came for me.""

"That was a coincidence, Layla. An accident."

"Why do you think you are here, Swan? Why do you think I came for you? There are no accidents, Swan."

She pulls over to the curb and cuts the engine. She reaches onto the jeep's back seat and brings up a cane carved with bejeweled faces of birds and men and demons. She twists its hawk head top and it opens to become a thin long dagger. She holds it towards me then twists it back into the cane head. "For later," she says. "Later we will become blood sisters."

I know now that Layla is mad as a hatter. And I am in a jeep with her and nobody knows where I am. Layla starts the engine and my mind shouts jump run now. Layla touches my knee, gently, not grabbing, and I can't move. She pulls back into the street. The traffic has thinned and although I don't know my way around Tulum I know for certain that we're going in the wrong direction.

"I'd like to go back to Casa Linda, Layla," I say. "I'm a little tired. I want to nap before the four o'clock session. I'm so looking forward to it."

"Why don't we go to my house instead? I have 76 solar panels and air conditioning. We can have a drink. We'll get to know each other a little."

"76 solar panels, wow," I say, thinking of Bridget's four.

"Bridget—you know Bridget—she's an engineer. She's very attentive to how I live. I don't need solar panels, of course. I can channel the sun." She closes her eyes, takes her hands off the steering wheel, and spreads her arms as if gathering its rays.

I grab the steering wheel. She opens her eyes and retakes it calmly.

Soon we're driving on a dirt car track paralleling the sea and jungle. There are no hotels, no cafes, no mud tents, no vendors. It is mid-afternoon and the sea is iridescent and the air is immaculate and Layla is driving scary fast. Our hair is flowing behind us in the wind we're creating. Layla looks over at me and laughs and for a moment I become one with the primal splendor around us and as I look back at her the word sociopath crosses my mind but I spit it out and laugh back. She lets go of the steering wheel and closes her eyes and instead of grabbing it I close mine.

We stop in front a giant gate that clearly tells people to stay out. I stand up from my seat and look around. We're in the middle of magnificent nowhere. "All this is mine, Swan. I own all of it. Here." She hands me a remote which I press and the gate swings open. "I could have commanded it to open but I'm saving my power for later," she says. I have crossed into that emotional state where disbelief is suspended, where the impossible seems possible. I look at her with dumbfounded assent and see that her eyes are laughing. She drives us through the gate. "Close, if you please, Swan."

We drive maybe a quarter of a mile and then veer off onto another car track. We pass a small white shack. A policeman armed like the one at the cave comes out. When he sees Layla he salutes.

"Where are we going?" I ask.

"I am taking you to my power place, Swan. I think it will be a power place for you, too."

The car track ends at a narrow path. Layla get out of the jeep. So do I.

"Leave your shoes," she says. "Come."

I discard my flip flops and follow her. We're walking on the smoothed tops of tree trunks set into wet ground crawling with water bugs. We pass a wall covered with hundreds of blue crabs. Humming birds dart in and out of Layla's red mane.

"This is like a fairy tale!" I say to her.

"Not a fairy tale. Reality. We're going to see if you're real, Swan Are you? Are you using your powers to see the truth, or are you using them to help men who want power over you. Power over me. Do you want truth, Swan?"

"I do, of course. I do."

As we walk the tree trunk stepping stones get further apart and being shorter than Layla I am not so much stepping as leaping from one to the next in her wake. The path is so narrow that spiky fronds scratch at my arms and head and I'm starting to feel panicky when suddenly the jungle opens onto what looks like a miniature lake. It has a dock that creaks and sways as Layla walks out on it. Without a word, she disrobes, dives, and vanishes under the water.

"This is a cenote, Swan," she calls to me from its middle. "It's fed from sweet underground springs. It has no bottom. It is very cold. Come. You must show Lord Kisin you are worthy."

I take my clothes off hastily and without hesitation I dive in. The water is freezing. I doggie paddle furiously to keep warm.

Layla swims further away from me and dives. She re-surfaces, rises high and flips backwards like a dolphin. She does this again then again and again before she finally stops near the lake's edge and shakes her hair.

"Now you," she says.

I know I can't thrust myself in the air like that, but I dive deep and when I turn my head up I rise towards the light as fast as some exotic water bird, then I am out of the water and arching my back and diving backwards like I'm a dolphin. It's like centrifugal force has seized me and is making me dive and leap and dive until it has had enough and I am floating on my back with the sun reaching through the jungle to find and warm my face. I see Guy de Guy and Hidalgo and they are laughing with delight from inside the sun and so I laugh too because I know they forgive me and are happy for me and love me. I feel at peace in a way I have never felt before. And I know that *this* is reality and all the sadness and remorse I have felt over their death is a false emotion. They are happy for me and love me. I could float like this forever.

"Swan."

I open my eyes. Layla is standing on the dock dressed. The sun is setting. How is that possible? I must have been floating for hours. I right myself and swim to the dock.

"Let's go to my hacienda," Layla says.

I dress silently and follow her over the tree stump stepping stones, past the blue crabs. The humming birds have become interested in me. They pause to peer into my eyes which must be refracting spears of sunlight before darting off.

"You saw something at the cenote, didn't you, Swan?" Layla says as we climb back in the Jeep and drive past the saluting guard.

"I did," I say.

"I knew you could see. But you have to know when you are seeing false spirits and when the spirits are true. I think you can do that," she says.

Nothing could make me think that the spirits I saw in the cenote were false. Guy de Guy and Hildago had visited me and released me from my terrible guilt. And as we drive into the dark jungle, I know that whatever baggage I had brought with me to Mexico was left behind in the care of the blue crabs and the fussing hummingbirds and the water of the cenote.

"You are free now, Swan. You are no longer safe. You are free."

Chapter 21

Full House

We drive for miles on a curving car track till we suddenly come out on a bluff peninsula high above the beach. A giant steel and glass geodesic dome is perched at the tip of the peninsula. Rows and rows of solar panels line a cliff above it.

"This is your house? I thought you lived with Hunter."

She parks the jeep between two black Escalades as if to indicate to me there are others waiting for us. She takes my hand and leads me on a footpath that runs along the bluff. I'm a little afraid, but that feeling is overwhelmed by the beauty all around us. The sea below and behind us marshlands that disappear into the horizon.

"Come," she says, pulling me into the domicile. "You have all the time in the world to look at the universe."

The setting sun is streaming in through portholes in the dome. Bridget is sitting in the living room with her boyfriend Amador. The tiny man with the diamond teeth and gun jumps down off his chair and holds his bejeweled cane towards me in greeting. Goliath is here too. But no Devil Dog. Devil Dog! I'd been too busy thinking about me to think about you. Please be safe and find your way back to me!

"Hey, Southie girlfriend," Bridget says. There's an ice bucket on a glass coffee table in front of her with a champagne bottle in it. She goes to a blue glass bar and brings back a stemmed flute and fills it. "Cristal," she says. "Do you know how expensive this stuff is? These guys drink it like beer. Your hair is all wet."

"We went swimming in the cenote," Layla answers for me.

"Layla thinks her ancestor's spirits live at the bottom," Bridget says, derisively, touching my glass with hers. "Cheers!"

I lift mine and sip. My first taste of really good champagne is delicious. The aftertaste is even better. "You've been to the cenote?"

"Why would I go to a cenote when I have the whole ocean to swim in? That's the difference between me and Layla," Bridget says.

"She's bewitched by the mysticism of this place. Tulum is a business opportunity, nothing more."

Layla goes up a circular stairway and I notice two tall, shaven-headed, tattoo covered men sitting at a gigantic slab dining table. The table is covered with champagne bottles and in the middle is a stack of money—hundred dollar bills—a foot high. Both men are wearing shoulder holsters. There is a machine pistol next to one of them. They are laughing uproariously and chugging Cristal straight from the bottle. The first to smack his empty bottle down on the table takes a handful of the bills from the stack.

"Come with me, Southie sister," Bridget says. She tugs me into a huge kitchen where two women—a beautiful young Mexican girl who is wearing only a bikini bottom and a Mayan hag in dirty whites—are feeding their faces from a counter full of meats.

"Out," Bridget says.

The old lady goes to a door that leads outside. The girl gulps down a piece of meat, pats her black hair, and starts past us.

Bridget stops her. "More," she says, holding up her empty glass.

The girl returns with a bottle of Cristal in an ice bucket then goes out into the dining room and puts her arms around one of the chuggers.

Goliath has followed us into the kitchen and is up on his hind legs snatching at the meat. Bridget takes him to the door, tosses a piece of meat out ahead of him, and closes the door behind him.

"So what do you think of our Layla?" Bridget asks. "I asked her to be extra nice to you. Was she?"

"I don't understand."

"Was she?"

I take a swig of Cristal and sit down on a stool at the table.

"Eat something," Bridget says. "You need a clear head. Do you know who Layla is?"

"She's descended from the seventeenth royal Mayan."

Bridget laughs. "She's royalty all right. She's the biggest drug dealer around here."

"What do you mean?"

"I *mean*, Southie sister, that Layla is one of the biggest drug dealers in Quinta Roo."

"Dick told me," I jerk my thumb towards the living room, "that your boyfriend, Amador was."

"Before Layla arrived Amador ran things here for me. I developed this turf before any of the glitz arrived. Layla convinced Amador and all the others—the meth cooks, the mescal pickers, the waiters in the hotels—that she's a goddess. She's got brass balls. I'll give her that. But she got careless and she let it get too big. Maybe it's Hunter's fault. It doesn't matter. This was the mess I came down to fix. Unfortunately, I was too late." She glances out at the dining room. "*Bigger* operators got wind of what we had going here. The Zetas. They've bought the two biggest hotels in Carmen del Playa. They say they'll work with me as long as Layla's out. But after her, it will be my turn. Plus, they want to bring heroin into the mix. I want no part of that. Since my days at Saint Marion I took an oath I never would. Heroin is a trashy drug. You do heroin to obliterate reality. What kind of a loser are you to want to do that?"

"I totally agree," I say and I slug down what's left in my glass and bang it on the counter. Bridget refills it and I take a long swig because I am in so far over my head that I'm clueless. "What are you going to do?" I slur.

"I'll try to work something out with them. I'm in too deep and their reach is too long to just walk away. And I've got Boston which will interest them. Here, eat this. You've got to stay sober."

"You're going to sell out Layla?"

"Believe me, girlfriend, she would sell me out in a heartbeat. Look what she's doing to Hunter!"

"What's she doing to Hunter?"

"She's planning to give him up to the Feds to get the IRS off her back.

"Feds? What Feds?"

"Your *friend* Dick."

"Dick and I are not technically *friends*."

"And that guy you spent the night with."

"And they're here to do *what*?" I ask blushing which I shouldn't be doing for Pete's sake since everyone in Tulum Playa has already heard my screams and seen me naked.

"To bring Layla down. And maybe more. I'm not sure yet what they know. I was hoping you could tell me."

I lay two fingers on the bridge of my nose and do an impromptu alternate-nostril breath to get a grip and I am about to ask Bridget to explain what she thinks I know when Layla comes through the kitchen door. She regards Bridget warily. She's changed into a turquoise diaphanous gown with slits in the shoulders to show off her terrible tattoo. She's wearing nothing underneath. For the first time I realize how powerful a beautiful body can be. I feel myself reeling in her presence. Maybe I'm wrong to cover mine up.

Layla pours herself a glass of Cristal. "Bridget, dear, Amador wants something. And he says, only *you* can give it to him." She smiles wickedly as Bridget leaves the room. "I'm sure she was giving you an earful."

I laugh nervously. I feel like a book getting squeezed between two Amazon book ends.

"Swan, you have to decide at some point in your life if you're going to be one of the big people or one of the little people." She pours the contents of her glass into the sink. "I don't drink while I'm working. Now is your time, Swan. I know what I am and we are about to find if you have the capacity to be one of the big people. You saw you could be this afternoon in the cenote. And I know what you saw at the ruins when Christine died. You saw me." She touches the hawk on her shoulder. "If you do what you need to do now you will be my blood sister. Those pissants out there Bridget is courting think they can bring me down. Me, a daughter of Maya. And you'll be next since they've seen we are blood sisters. We can't let that happen, can we, Swan? And do you know how they're going to bring me down? Do you know how?"

I shake my head no. I am terrified.

"I got you out of jail this afternoon, Swan. No one else could have done that. Not Hunter. Not Bridget. Not your boyfriend. Not even your precious Dick. This is Mexico. In Mexico you are guilty until proven innocent. How could you ever prove you weren't stealing that ceremonial dagger?"

"How do you know about that?"

"The dagger is mine. It called me. You would have rotted in jail until your parents came looking for you."

"My parents are dead," I say.

"So you would have died there."

"I *know*," I say. When I'm out of my mind with fear, I babble. "God, thank you so much Layla. All afternoon I wanted to thank you. Honestly, I don't know what I would have done if you hadn't come. Those women. With their babies. They begged me to buy them water. I've never seen anything so pathetic. And they stank, Layla. They thought I was lying about not having money even though I turned out my pant pockets and I think they were planning to search me, you know what I'm saying, when you came." I take her hand. I'm not sure but I think I would have kissed it if she hadn't pulled it away.

"I helped you, Swan. Isn't that right?"

"Yes."

She places her hands over mine on the counter and looks me up and down like she did at the ruins with her brilliant turquoise eyes that aren't lenses. Her red hair is touching my face and up close it seems like a fiery halo and her body is naked under her turquoise gown and the ferocious tattoo on her shoulder is sneering redder than her hair and I feel like I'm going to faint because she really is some kind of terrible goddess.

"I've done you a favor to prove my good intentions towards you, Swan. And now it's *your* turn to prove your good intentions towards *me*."

I feel like I'm going to be sick and it's not the champagne. I lick my lips. They feel like they're cracking my mouth is so dry. "What do you want, Layla?"

She smiles and releases me. "I knew I could count on you, Swan. We are really so alike that refusing me would be like refusing *yourself*."

"Yes."

"The Zetas have taken over Carmen del Playa and now they want to swallow up my Tulum. They've put their people in the government and before long they'll take away my police. They've already demanded a vig. Can you imagine? From *me*! Of course, I refused to pay. They'll squeeze me until there's nothing left and then, well... But who belongs in Tulum more than I do? Tulum is mine."

Layla's switch from goddess to harried businesswoman is like a cold shower on a January morning. For a moment I feel at a complete loss. But the longer she dwells on the details of her problem the more I feel at home. Sobering words begin to appear in my mind. Sociopath. Insane person. Drug dealer. When I ask again: "What do you want, Layla?" I am stalling for time till I have the courage to tell her I won't do it.

"You must focus, Swan, focus. It's a matter of focus."

"Does this have something to do with yoga?" I ask. "Dick says yoga is about focus."

"Yoga? I'm not talking about yoga. I mean that we—you and I—have to shift the focus of the little investigation that's at our door from *me* and that stupid son of a bitch Hunter with his harem of trolls and his loose tongue onto the Zetas from Carmen del Playa."

"So what do you want me to do?"

"Call off the hounds! Call them off! Tell them I will close down Savas Hanna and help them bag the Zetas." She gestures toward the dining room where the drinking game is obviously over because one of the players is passed out on the table with his money clutched in his hand, which the bikini-bottomed woman is casually plucking one bill at a time.

"I know how these things work a little, I'm from Southie, remember, and it's probably too late if they've already bought the local judges. So it won't matter what Dick and Mark find out about them."

I picture Christine toppling off the cliff and Karen with a needle in her arm. I hope that some of the blood Dick scraped up was Layla's.

And speaking of Dick, he always shows up at the last minute to save me. So where exactly is he? And Mark. His motive is vengeance more than justice. He'll be like a bull dog with its jaws clamped on Layla's leg until he finds out who's responsible for the murder of his wife.

"What happens if I can't get them to do what you want?" I ask.

"*Of course* you can get them to do it," she says. "You'll find a way. You have the power."

Power. See, I've never understood why anyone would want power over anyone else. Power implies control and I have enough trouble controlling myself, don't you? I was growing weary of Layla and her fantastic demands. Even if she does look like a fabulous fairy tale goddess in that see-through get-up.

"And what if I just *won't?*" I ask, standing up and sitting right back down because I'm a little drunk but also tired of everything that's happened. Tired of thinking about poor Christine and Karen, tired of finding out that the serenity business is a front for drugs, tired that a car bomb was meant for me and Dick, tired of losing my beautiful dog who is probably wandering in the jungle looking for me, fighting off who-knows-whats. "Maybe I don't think it's the right thing to do. So maybe I won't."

"Ah, Swan, dear Swan, haven't I shown you who I am? Haven't I shown you who you're dealing with? Of course you will do what I want you to do if you ever want to hear this again." Layla takes a cell phone off a charger on the counter and dials a number. Someone picks up and Layla says, "*Trae el perrito*" and she hands the phone to me and I put it to my ear.

"Hello," I say and freeze when I hear a dog barking.

"Is that....?"

"Yes, Swan, that's your little Devil Dog," she says, picking the phone up off the floor as I run out of the kitchen.

Chapter 22

Joy Ride

I run through the living room and out the glass front door. Bridget gets off Amador's lap and runs out after me.

"What happened?" she shouts and snatches at my hand. "Where do you think you're going?"

"I've got to get out of here."

"You don't have a car."

"I'll walk," I say, running down the path that runs along the cliff.

The geo dome is gleaming with light and I see some steps that lead down to the beach. If I walk on the beach eventually I'll come to Tulum Playa. When I get to the bottom I see that the tide is in and the beach is a sliver and the water is lapping at the dunes behind it. I climb back up the stairs and start walking on the car track toward the jungle.

"Wait," Bridget yells. "I'll take you. You can't go by yourself. You'll never make it."

She runs back toward the house. I am stumbling along weeping when Bridget roars up next to me in a dune buggy. Goliath is with her. She drives in the sand so close beside me that I finally get in.

"It didn't go well. I didn't think it would."

"She has Devil Dog," I say.

"Where?"

"I don't know. She dialed some number and I heard him barking. My poor little dog!"

"I told you she would betray you. She'll betray anyone if she doesn't get what she wants."

Goliath, who is sitting behind us, starts whining. It's a sympathy whine. I pet him and feel jealous that Bridget has Goliath but I don't have Devil Dog.

The buggy has headlights and a spot on the roll bar and we tear through the jungle and pass the guard shack which is lit up but deserted. When we get to the gate Bridget pulls out her own wand and opens it.

"She lets you come and go whenever you please?"

"I don't work for Layla. I thought I explained that to you."

"Where's the guard?"

"He probably went home for dinner. He'll be back. He sleeps there."

"Dick said I should expect the opposite in Mexico of everything I'm used to. "

"He's right. This isn't Southie, Swanson."

"But everything is so *topsy turvy* here. Non-stop."

"It's all what you're used to, Swanson. You want to know the truth? I thrive on it."

"I don't get it. How can you all think that dealing drugs is not a big a deal?"

"This is Mexico, Swanson. Most of the people who take drugs here have their reasons. Some are religious. Some are cultish. Some are violent. Changing your reality isn't considered evil here like it is back home. It's the tourists who are the wild card."

"But drugs are illegal."

"Only because Mexico has to stay friends with the States. If it didn't have to, I guarantee Mexico wouldn't give a damn. It barely does now except for show. The Mayans, the Aztecs, the Toltecs, they're ancient civilizations that used drugs to figure out how to stay on the right side of the fickle universe. Half the people in Mexico still have no idea who's responsible for the sun coming up in the morning."

"Doesn't that scare you?"

"Why should it scare me?"

"The deck you've been playing with has gotten stacked against you, right? Wouldn't you prefer to be someplace where there are laws, rules, taboos, for you to hide behind?"

"If you're playing for high stakes there's nothing to hide behind. Everything, everywhere, is live or die. In your line of work you must know that. Jesus, what's worse than people getting divorced? See? That's what's happening here. Me and Layla are getting divorced and I'm going to marry the highest bidder. If he doesn't want to pay my price, then too bad for him or too bad for me."

This is mind boggling stuff and we ride for a long time in silence. The sky is swimming with stars that slowly extinguish as we enter Tulum Playa with its glowing hotels and cafes. Bridget stops in front of Casa Linda and signs for me to get out.

"You're going back?"

"Yes. More Zetas will arrive tonight. I can't leave that snake Layla alone with them."

"How can you be so calm, Bridget?"

"I've lived this way since I was fourteen years old."

Even though we were Southie sisters, it seemed we grew up on different planets.

"Then can you help me with something? As my Southie sister? I don't know how to play this game. I just want to get out of here alive with my dog."

"What is it you want?"

"Help me find Devil Dog,"

Goliath has taken my place next to her. He licks her face on cue.

"He's my only friend."

"Why don't you tell me what you know before I leave?"

"About what?"

"About *everything*." She looks hard at me then she shakes her head and laughs. "Either you really *don't* know what's going on or you're a very good actress. I'll see what I can do about your little dog, *chica*. You'll owe me. The gate's open. Goodnight."

She takes the dune buggy in a tight turn and roars back toward the jungle.

Chapter 23

I Don't Iguana Know

When we arrived in Tulum, Dick told me that it was better to stay in a place like Bridget's because electricity was precious and leaving a light footprint was a life lesson.

"I'd rather have a *light* right now than a light footprint," I grumble.

The flagstone path from the gate to the hacienda is treacherously dark. I try to see where Mark's aerie should be but it's so dark it's like it's not there. I'm groping for the kitchen porch which I'm sure I should have reached by now when my right leg bumps into something large and scaly. I teeter and fall sideways to avoid it and land on a cactus. My right arm feels like it's been raked by nails and my ankle smarts and when I touch it where it's burning I feel blood. Then I hear a swish and I realize what bumped my other ankle.

"Stop it! Stop it!" I yell at the darkness. I hear palms swoshing and claws tapping flagstones. The creature is as scared of me as I am of it. But I'm down and wounded and the iguana has gotten off unscathed. I lay down where I am and cry. I don't care where I am or whether I'm safe. If Devil Dog was here, he would have taken the iguana down! I want my dog. Where is my dog?

Suddenly someone is walking towards me shining a bright LED light in my eyes.

"You're *bleeding*!" Mark says.

"Just a little."

"It's not just a little! Didn't I tell you not to get on the wrong side of an iguana?"

"I was looking for the *right* side but I couldn't see it in the *dark*."

"We have to get that taken care of right now."

He bends down, scoops me up in his arms and carries me up the stairs to my room. Very gently, he sets me down on the futon I haven't slept on yet then goes back down the stairs. I hear him rummaging through the kitchen. He comes back with a bowl of water, a bar of soap, a roll of paper towels, and a red bottle of something.

"Vinegar is all I could find," he says.

"You've got to be kidding."

"It'll work as an antiseptic. We're in the middle of a jungle. We have to improvise."

"There are pharmacies in town."

"It's a long way to town. It's vital to clean a wound right away. I've seen guys lose a leg because, well, just because. Be still. It will burn but so what."

"Losing a leg? What are you talking about?" I ask, as he washes my arm and ankles and pours vinegar on them.

"Afghanistan. Herat province. Very nasty shit. "

"Oh." I don't know the first thing about Mark except that his wife was killed and someone down here is responsible and that we spent a fabulous night together. And now this grisly tidbit.

"What happened to you this morning at the ruins? All of a sudden you disappeared."

"Would you rather we both got arrested?"

"So you knew I got arrested and you didn't try to get me out?"

"I couldn't get you out but I was there watching when Layla did. I would have rescued you from her but she lost me in traffic."

I digest this piece of information as Mark finishes cleaning and bandaging my wounds with strips of bed sheet. I'm feeling a wave of appreciation for him that I have to stifle because if Bridget doesn't come through for me I'll have to find a way to make Mark and Dick shift focus from Layla to the Zetas so I can get my dog back.

I'm not good at manipulating people and everyone around me is playing games I don't play. A wave of anxiety comes over me and instead of taking a deep breath and trying to cope I attack Mark. I mean, I know that stinks but my leg is killing me. "You're a liar. You didn't tell me you're a narc. I'll bet everything you told me last night you made up."

"A *narc*? Just because Regan was a narc you assume I'm one? And I don't lie."

"Well, if you're not a narc, what are you?"

"I'm a PI. Like Dick."

"I saw your Boston police badge. You're lying."

"I'm on leave. They think I'm a loose cannon because of Regan. They're probably right. Finished," he says. He puts a finger to his lips, kisses it and pats my leg. "Calm down, Swanson. I'm probably the only person here you can trust."

"Layla kidnapped Devil Dog, Mark. I have to find him."

"She wants money, right? She's going to need a lot of it. She's in very deep shit and just because she's here doesn't mean that she won't have to come back to Boston. Holding a dog for ransom. That's new."

"She doesn't want money."

"Well then, what?"

"She wants things to go her way."

"And what way would that be?"

"She wasn't specific."

I have my legs on Mark's lap and he's stroking them, when loud footsteps clomp up the stairs.

"Who else is here?" I whisper as Hunter and Dick enter my room. "You!" I say to Dick. "And you!"

"Nice to see you, too, Swanson."

"What happened to you this afternoon, Dick? What did you do with that dagger? I went to jail over that stupid knife. They think we're tomb looters."

"The dagger is in a safe place, Swanson. And the DNA samples I scraped are in a lab right now in Boston. I had to drive all the way to Cancun to get the samples on a Fedex jet but I tracked the package and it's already there. I should have bought Fedex stock when it was at 18. I'm sorry about you going to jail, Swanson, but I was busy. You managed to get out, didn't you?"

I gesture at Hunter who hasn't even acknowledged I'm in the room. "What's he doing here?"

"Hunter had a visit this afternoon from some gentlemen from

Carmen del Playa, didn't you Hunter?"

Hunter nods.

"He wants to cut a deal with us. Do you think we can arrange something, Mark?"

Whoa. This is fresh. A couple of PIs, well, if Mark isn't lying to me, with no clout at all here gaming one of the bad guys. Dick always manages to surprise me.

"They've kidnapped Devil Dog, Dick. He's gone."

"You mean *dog*napped, Swanson. Where is he?"

"If I knew where he was he wouldn't be *gone*, would he? I want my dog back. And I want to go home."

"We can't go home yet, Swanson. We have to find out who murdered Christine and Karen."

"Well, if you're sure they were murdered that's a no-brainer. I say the Mayan Goddess did it. Hunter should know."

"Just a damn minute," Hunter says. "I came to you guys in good faith. I'm willing to close Savas Hanna down and help you bag a big one. The Zetas are going to muscle in on the drug trade here. Layla is small potatoes, and I know someone else you may be very interested in. But I want to make it clear right now. I don't know anything about any murders and neither does my off-her-rocker wife."

"Let's not forget Regan," Mark says. "She's why I'm here. What exactly do you mean that you know someone else, Hunter?"

"Get me a deal with the IRS and she's yours."

"She?"

"This is all going to be moot pretty soon, isn't it?" I say. "The Zetas are going to smash everyone in the vicinity, probably including us. I saw two of them at Layla's. That's where I spent the afternoon. Actually, three of them. That midget you say is a Zeta hit man was there too. I mean, they're the big game. Let's change the focus onto them."

Dick looks at me curiously. "Where is this coming from, Swanson?"

"I just thought of it actually," I lie, rolling my yoga pants down over my wounded legs.

"So what's the plan," Mark asks.

"I can pretty much guarantee whose blood is going to show up from the scrapings I took at the cave and there was dried blood on the dagger too. You'd think they'd keep a sacred object clean. But that just means that a murder occurred. It doesn't have the murderer's signature on it. You almost always have to catch a murderer red-handed."

"Wouldn't the murderer's DNA be all over what you scraped up?" I ask.

"Just because someone was there, doesn't mean they did it. They could plead they cut their hand during some ritual. And my DNA is probably all over everything too. I forgot to buy gloves."

"So what's the plan?" Mark repeats.

Hunter has been pacing nervously. "Look, whatever you want to do let's get it done. I'm on your side. For now. This murder stuff is freaking me out. I mean, I know that my acting nonchalant when bodies were piling up didn't look good. But you've got to understand. I try to create a bubble for my clients. Serenity is my business."

"What's the *plan*, god damn it," Mark repeats.

"I say if we find Devil Dog, we find answers. Whoever has Devil Dog is up to their eyeballs in the murders," I say.

"Well then let's go to Layla's," Mark says. "She's the one who's holding Devil Dog hostage. She knows where he is. I don't buy this apologist's bullshit. He's obviously one of these guys who screws around on his wife but still's madly in love with her".

"Bugger off," Hunter says.

We all look at Dick who is balancing on the back two legs of a chair, tapping the tips of his fingers together in that completely annoying way he has. It's so quiet I can hear the iguanas rustling the palms.

Finally he rights himself and smiles. "'The plays the thing wherein we catch the conscience of the King.'"

I sit up. I know this one by heart. I was in the high school play for god's sake. And he's misquoting poor Hamlet.

"It's '*I* catch the conscience of the King, Dick," I say, authoritatively, "Not *we*."

"Ha!" Dick says.

"What?" Mark asks, his face distraught.

"Never mind. But look it up, Dick. I'm right."

"I'll prove you wrong later," Dick says. "Now, we do a sting. It's the only way. We catch them in the act and bam! We're all over them."

"A sting could work," Mark says.

"You in?" Dick asks Hunter.

"Yeah, okay. What's the plan? Who's the bait?"

I go through the members of the yoga retreat. There are two blond beauties left and that Mark clone who never says anything.

I'm just about to volunteer the Grace with the collagen-enhanced lips when I realize the three guys are looking me.

"*What?*"

"Swanson, you're the bait. Go up to your platform, Mark, and get the telephoto."

"And the guns," Mark says, bolting down the stairs.

"Not good. He's too wired," Dick says as we watch Mark take the three flights of steps to his aerie two at a time. "By the way, Swanson, that was Hamlet."

"I know the quote, Dick. I was *in* the play. I was *Ophelia* for three nights and two matinees."

"Talk about miscasting! You can tell me all about it on the flight home."

He thought there was going to be a flight home with me on it. That was hopeful. "Oh, I definitely will. But right now I'd like to know, why me? Why not one of the tall look-a-likes?"

"We don't know if we can trust them," Dick says. "And we know we can trust you."

I blush, thinking that I want to help Layla deflect suspicion from her so I can retrieve my dog.

"I want to make a phone call before I walk the plank. My cell is conked. Give me yours."

"Who do you want to call?"

"My uncles."

Chapter 24

There's No Place Like Home

Dick, contrary to all his Luddite tendencies, arranged to have his Android work in Mexico. I could kick myself for not doing the same.

I dial the French prefix, then Uncle Joe's number in Paris. If a woman answers, I tell myself, I will hang up because I don't want to hear how happy in love he is. Although that's really stupid. Uncle Joe—Uncle Stevie for that matter, too—always has a woman around. After ten rings he finally picks up.

"*Le Haut Dog!*" he says, "*Bonjour! Voulez-vous faire une reservation?*"

"Uncle Joe!" I yell into the phone.

"Swanson, oh my god, is that you?! Stevie, it's Swanson."

I can hear plates banging and lots of laughter and talking in the background. It's the late night crowd at the diner. I want to cry because I'm not with them.

"Where are you, Swanson?"

"I'm in Tulum. That's in Mexico," I add in case he didn't know. Actually, I didn't know until about two weeks ago where Tulum was myself.

"What's the matter, Swanson. You sound *terrible*," he says.

"Do I?" I snurf. I'm crying. Damn. I can never hide anything from Uncle Joe. "I'm on a yoga retreat."

"Well, no wonder you sound like hell. *Stevie*, she's in *Mexico*. On a *yoga* retreat! What do you need, Swanson? Do you need money?"

"No, I don't need money. I just wanted to hear your voices. To tell you where I am."

In case someone has to come and claim my body, I want to say. Jeez, maybe Uncle Joe and Stevie and even Dick for pete's sake are right: I should get married if for no other reason than somebody will know where I am.

To claim my body. I shiver.

"No, everything is honkey doory here, Uncle Joe. I'm getting quite flexible. You wouldn't believe what your body can do until you ask it." Which is an incredibly silly thing to say, but I can't say what I really want to say which is: I miss you guys. Why did you move to Paris? Shouldn't family always make a point of staying in the same state, if not the same city?

Uncle Joe chortles. "I've asked my body to do quite a few new things lately. These French women, Swanson, you wouldn't believe it! Well, you had a French boyfriend, so maybe you would."

And we're both silent, remembering just how unlucky in love I am.

"Well, there's nothing really to report. Just hi and I'm staying at the Casa Linda here in Tulum if you need anything. That's C-A-S-A L-I-N-D-A."

"We don't need anything, Swanson. But let us know if you do."

I was ready to hang up when it occurred to me to ask, "Hey, Uncle Joe, do you remember somebody from Southie named Regan McGonigle? It was a couple of years ago. She was killed the day before she was to testify against a bunch of drug dealers. She was a narc."

"Regan McGonigle? Regan McGonigle? No. Can't say that I do. Hey, wait, Stevie says he does. Calm down, Stevie, for god's sake. You're going to have a heart attack. I worry about him, Swanson, honest to god. He's so excitable. He's a *hearttackwaiter*. That's a good word. Hey, I'm going to send it in to Merriam-Webster. I think they'll go for this one. No charge!"

I hear the scrunching sound as the phone changes hands and Stevie's heavy breathing on the other line.

"Swanson? You there? Swanson, what's going on down there? Does someone there know Regan McGonigle?"

The urgency in his voice frightens me. As if I wasn't already

ready to pee my pants, what with being bait in a sting operation and all. "What's the matter, Uncle Stevie?"

"What do you know about Regan McGonigle?" he asks me.

"Nothing, except that she's from Southie, she was married to this guy, she was an undercover cop and she was going to testify against this drug gang and she got knifed the night before. Her husband is here now trying to find out who murdered her." I was running out of breath.

"She played with a tough crowd," Uncle Stevie says. "Drug dealers."

"Well, I *know* that."

"Are you hanging out with her friends? Don't hang out with her friends. You never know with those people, who's side they're on. They're like vicious animals. Anybody else from Southie down there?"

"Just everyone else on the yoga retreat," I say, not wanting to tell him that a third of them were now dead.

"Just be careful. The woman that McGonigle girl was going to testify against is rumored to be in Mexico now. Just keep your wits about you. And keep your eyes and ears open. There was a rumor that she escaped to Mexico."

I could feel my heart beating right through my *Le Haut Dog* tee shirt. It *was* Layla.

"And Swanson?"

"Yes, Uncle Stevie?"

"Take care of yourself, kid. And if you do run into that drug lady down there…"

"Yes?"

"She's not a nice girl. Run like hell."

Chapter 25

The Play's the Thing

There's this balancing pose in yoga called the tree. You stand on one leg, the other foot touching the standing leg, either around the ankle or the shin; if you're really flexible, the thigh. Knee out. Hands in prayer position first, then when you find your *drishti* –a point, speck of dust to focus on—hands raise over your body, clasped with index fingers pointing up. And finally you spread your arms out like the branches of a tree.

It's the perfect position, I am told, for times of great stress because what's more powerful than standing and doing nothing when the people around you are swirling like madmen. Or madwomen?

I do it now on Casa Linda's kitchen porch while Mark, Dick and Hunter are inside planning the sting to catch Christine and Karen's murderers. It's about six thirty and the sun is starting to dip. Tulum and Boston are in the same time zone. It's hard for me to grasp that just because the weather is hot doesn't mean the days are any longer than they are in Boston, which in November are getting shorter and drearier.

"Swanson? You coming in?" Mark asks from the door.

I fall out of the tree. "Sure, sure. I just had to get my bearings."

"You okay?" he asks. He comes up behind me and starts massaging my shoulders. Just an hour ago when he was cleaning my iguana and cactus wounds, I thought he was possibly the kindest man in the world. Now I am so keyed up I have to force myself not to cringe when he touches me. He must have known Layla was the woman Regan was going to testify against. Why would he keep that from me?

"I'm good," I say, shaking him off.

He turns me around and keeps his hands on my shoulders. "When this is all over, maybe we can go on a real date. When we get back to Boston, you know? I really like your company, Swanson."

"Absolutely. I know just where we can go."

"We just have to get through this." He starts massaging me again, and I shake him off.

"I'm a little on edge," I say.

"Gotcha. The sooner we get this done, the sooner we can go back home. You should come in and see what we cooked up."

For some reason that conjures up an image of me sitting in a cannibal's pot.

I duck into the kitchen. "You want to fill me in?" I ask.

"We have it figured out," Dick says. "Hunter thinks the reason that these girls were killed was because they were getting too close to knowing how Savas Hanna financed its operations. Hunter admits he may have told them something when they were in bed and that both Christine and Karen may have told Layla what they knew to get her to leave Hunter."

"Which he would never do because he was so much *in love* with Layla," I say sarcastically. "Which is why he was in bed with these *other* women."

"Don't judge me, Swanson," Hunter says. "It's an occupational hazard. You've never known sexual power over another person. It's better than any drug."

I bristle at his assessment of my sexual prowess. "What*ever*."

"So, now, Swanson, we're going to put you in a position where it looks as if you and Hunter are getting too close and see who comes out of the woodwork to wack you," Dick says. "Get it?"

"Got it."

"We'll have your back, don't worry."

"I'm not worried at all," I lie. "But tell me, since you don't have jurisdiction here or anything, how exactly are you going to bring her in? And where is this little play going to take place?"

"At the ruins, of course."

"Of course."

"At midnight."

The witching hour. "I'll be ready."

"Don't worry," Mark says, "I've got your back."

"Right. Now if you gentlemen will excuse me," I pull at the ends of the xxxxl pink *Le Haut Dog* tee shirt, "I'm going to change into something a little more comfortable."

Something, I think, that I wouldn't mind being caught dead in.

Chapter 26

I'm Going to Wash That Fear Right Out of My Hair

I go to my room and gather up my toiletries, a headlight and one of the towels and robes that Bridget has laid out for me, then head to the outdoor shower. I can't remember when I bathed last. Well, if you count scrubbing off that yellow mud in the ocean this morning. Since then, I've been in jail, I've been swimming in a cenote with a drug kingpin—or is it queenpin?—doing back flips like a dolphin, communing with blue crabs and drinking Cristal in a hot bed of criminals. Oh, yeah, and my dog was kidnapped. This has certainly turned into a relaxing yoga retreat. I definitely need a shower. One time Dick told me that I had to learn to control my emotions because predators can smell fear. Well, I have a lot of fear on me and I probably need to wash it off.

The shower is in the back of the big three story building and I make my way there adjusting my headlight so I don't fall again. The shower is in a wooden stall with a jungle rain shower head. Wood planks make a natural drain on the floor. Bridget, that wonderful woman, has put out several different kinds of beautiful smelling soap. A little solar powered light softly illuminates the shower area.

I take off my headlight, toss my flip flops, peel off my rank yoga pants and the phenomenally unbecoming tee shirt and drop them on the floor. I pull the scrunchie out of my hair and shake my head, feeling for maybe the first time in my life the pleasure of my naked body. Why did I have to wait till the evening I might die to experience this? The possibility of death is making me appreciate life. It's a cliché you can hear a million times but until it happens to you the truth behind the cliché never registers.

I turn the water on and wait a minute before I step under the shower head. The water temperature is like the ocean—not too hot, just a little cool, so it feels reviving. The cactus scratches on my arm and the wounds where the iguana raked me smart and burn and ground me into the here and now. I let the water run over my body and pick out the gardenia—thank you, Bridget!—soap and lather myself. Then I shampoo my hair. And finally I stand under the water, letting it rinse me off. Letting it rinse off all my fear.

Sometimes at home when I shower, Devil Dog would come into the bathroom and pull at the curtain because he wanted to play. I sob. I have to accept the fact that I may never see Devil Dog again and I feel my heart breaking. When Uncle Joe and Uncle Stevie gave him to me two years ago "for protection" I thought they were crazy. How could a little stumpy dachshund ever protect me I thought then. I never took into account that there were other things besides bad men that I might need protection from. There is, for example, my own self-imposed loneliness.

I turn off the shower and towel off and when I turn around to grab my robe, I see someone staring at me. My mouth opens but no scream comes out.

"Sorry, Swanson," Mark says. "I don't mean to frighten you."

"I'm a little tense. What do you want, Mark?" I pull the robe tightly around me. All the pleasure I was feeling in my body dissipates.

"Dick and I leaving now. That's all I came to tell you."

"Great. Okay. See you later. And how am I supposed to get there?"

"Hunter will take you as if it's a romantic outing. We think Hunter is being followed all the time, so whoever is following him will follow you and Hunter to the ruins and… "

"I get it. Terrific plan. Now if you don't mind, I want to meditate and this seems to be the only place with even a smidgen of privacy."

"Are you mad at me, Swanson?"

The first time I met Layla she called me Swan and said swans were magical birds because they could see. I know now what she was talking about. I feel as if I was blind up until now, but now I can see everything clearly and I know that Mark, whatever else he is, is on my side.

"Go away, Mark. Please. I just want to be alone."

"Okay. Great. We'll talk later. Okay?"

"Righto. Here, take this," I hand him the headlamp. "I don't think I need it anymore."

Chapter 27

A Good Friend is Hard to Find

Of course I can kick myself for giving Mark my headlamp once I start back to the hacienda. It's a moonless night and I can't see a damned thing. So much for "seeing." I shuffle my feet along so if there is an iguana in the path, I won't stumble over it. A light pops on in the hacienda ahead of me, blinding me even more.

Shuffle, shuffle, finally I make it to the porch and open the kitchen door. Bridget is inside, making guacamole.

"There you are, girlfriend," she smiles. "Right on time."

Goliath almost knocks me over, paws on my shoulders, licking me.

"Get off her Goliath!" Bridget commands.

"It's okay," I say. "Hey, I'm surprised to see you back here."

Bridget hands me the treat bag. "Give him these. He'll eat them then leave you alone. Dogs are much simpler than humans. They're loyal to the hand that feeds them."

I give Goliath a treat and put the rest of the bag in my robe pocket to dole out to him later if he jumps me. I take a seat at the counter, which has a glass mosaic peace sign on the front, homage to Tulum's hippie past, I suppose. It's so funny how all the mystical stuff of hippiedom found a home in Tulum right next to all the Mayan mystical stuff.

"I'm officially starved, so if you're serving that guacamole, I say, yes, thank you."

Bridget laughs. "It's good to see people from home, isn't it?"

"I know. Even if we don't have any history together. Except one field hockey game that neither of us really remembers. Dick says…"

"Your good buddy Dick."

"Yes, him. Dick knows everyone in Southie."

"Does he? I knew I'd seen him before yesterday."

"Well, Dick spent a lot of time in Vietnam and he says that one of the things that kept him sane was hearing a Southie accent now and then in the jungle. Like in the middle of a rice paddie, he would hear some trooper dropping his r's, *pahking thea cah in Hahvahd yahd* and he was home."

"Imagine that. A Southie accent in the jungle. It's funny I never caught *his* accent."

"It's there sometimes. It comes out when he's stressed. Don't you miss that sometimes?" "Hearing the Southie accent?"

"May I?" I ask, pulling the bowl of guacamole towards me.

Bridget pulls it back. "Wait." She rummages in a drawer and pulls out a plastic bag full of white grains and stirs the contents into the mix. "Secret ingredient. Makes mine *special*. It's Mary Lawlor's guacamole recipe."

"Sugar, right?" I ask. "Sugar makes everything better. Maybe it's the Southie in us."

"Wait, sorry. Almost forgot. Here." Bridget opens a bag of blue corn chips and pours them into a bowl.

I devour the chips and guacamole as if I haven't eaten in a week. And come to think of it, I haven't. Well, two days. Same thing, basically.

"I don't hear Southie much anymore," I say. "Everyone's trying to lose their accent. They want to talk like the freakin' weatherman."

"Family though. You must have lots of family."

"No. My only family moved to France."

"Is that right?"

Bridget seems interested and I smile. It's nice to have a friend. Or at least, as Dick would say, to hear Southie in the middle of the jungle. It's *friendly*.

"It means a lot to me that you're here, Bridget. This place is a like a snake pit."

"Depends."

"Well, I probably shouldn't say this …I mean, you've been so nice to me…" I can't shut up all of a sudden. I feel like I had a couple of drinks. "Is like *everyone* here involved in drugs?"

"As a matter of fact, yes," Bridget says. "And I'm really tired of the little games you've been playing with me, Swanson. I gave you a chance to tell me what you know. You didn't. So it's lights out."

It seems as if there are three or four Bridgets right now, and I struggle to keep one in focus. "Bridget," I fight to keep from slurring, but I have to ask before I pass out, because I know I'm about to. "What did you find out about Devil Dog? Let's go get him right noooowwwwwww…."

My head thunks down on the counter. I'm passed out but still aware of what's going on around me. I remember that Uncle Stevie described his colonoscopy like that. And that thought strikes me funny, so I laugh, kind of a snorting laugh because my face is in the guacamole. Whatever anesthesia they gave my Uncle Stevie for his colonoscopy Bridget put in my snack. I want to ask her ""What's the secret ingredient in Mary Lawlor's guacamole, girlfriend?" but my mouth feels welded shut.

"Amador, get her out of here," I hear Bridget say through a tub of green slimy guacamole.

I think I'm saying, "Where are you taking me?" But what comes out is *blub, blub, blub.*

I feel two men picking me up and carrying me down the flagstone path. "Wait a minute," Bridget says, "she looks disgusting." She walks next to me and wipes my face with her apron. Say what you want about Southie chicks, we are very clean. I try to nod my head by way of thanks. "Stop her from flopping around like that. People will think she's drugged."

"Devil Dog," I moan. "Devil Dog."

"Get her in the car and get her out of here before those morons come back. And for pity's sake, hurry up."

Chapter 28

All She Wants to Do is Ride Around… Bridget?

The two men dump me in the rear seat of a black Escalade. They jump in the front and I see, out of one slitted eye, Bridget and Goliath get in. She says something in Spanish and we speed down the road for about a hundred yards then stop.

"Damn these tourists," Bridget says. "They're everywhere!"

I feel a slight breeze on my stomach. My robe is open. Robe. I didn't have a chance to change from the shower. I feel powerless to do anything about the open robe. I try to drag my hand to my hair to see if I have a towel around it, but my hand isn't obeying orders at the moment either. Why did I bother to buy all these cute new Lululemon clothes if I never get a chance to wear them?

"*Madre de Dios, Hector, usa tu cabeza,*" Bridget yells at the guy who's driving. "Get off the road! Drive on the beach."

Hector protests in Spanish, but Bridget yells, "Shut up! *Mueve!*" and I feel the SUV jump off the road onto the sand.

"This will destroy my car," he says in English.

"You will have more than your car destroyed if we don't get to the ruins quickly. That shit wears off in an hour."

What shit? Oh, the shit she put in the guacamole! The anesthesia. That's right. Uncle Stevie said he was up and around and in need of a hot dog in less than an hour. What does it matter if I'm awake or not?

"So we do it when she's awake. Who cares?" I hear Amador say.

"I care. She's a Southie."

And….so what? I think. Damn, I hate drugs. It feels like my thoughts are trapped in a foggy tunnel and can't find their way out.

The SUV is zooming over the sand. We must be down by the water, I hear it spattering the bottom of the SUV, and I feel the SUV lose its grip on the shifting sand and we swerve back and forth as the driver feels for something solid to drive on. A steady stream of Spanish curses comes from the front seat.

Bridget says something in Spanish and the cursing stops.

After about ten minutes the driver turns the car left and we climb through some rough bush which scratches at the SUV and the cursing starts again and we jump uphill until it feels as if we are on paved road again.

"*Gracias Dios*," Hector says.

"Shut up," Bridget says. "*Dios* has nothing to do with this."

"Señora Layla says…"

"I don't care what mumbo jumbo Señora Layla tells you. She doesn't pay you. I do."

The SUV drives quickly over the bumpy road before coming to a sudden stop. The rear door opens and the two men drag me out.

"Cover her up," Bridget commands.

Which they kind of do. At least, I can't feel the breeze on my chest anymore. The taller of the two, Amador I think, heaves me over his shoulder and we walk somewhere. Goliath keeps nipping at my robe and Amador kicks him. The blood rushing to my head clears my foggy vision and I watch upside down as I'm carried up a flight of stone steps and down another to a familiar looking place. It's the cave overlooking the cliff. Sonofabitch! They're going to kill me just like they killed Christine and Karen! But wait—the thought pushes through the sludge in my brain— why isn't Layla here? Didn't *Layla* kill them because of what they knew about her involvement in the drug trade? Nothing makes sense. I have the funny thought that I would like to know what the hell is going on before I die. Like why does *Bridget* want to kill me? Aren't we Southie girlfriends?

Southie. Southie. *SOUTHIE!* OMG! I see now, I wish this seeing stuff had kicked in a little sooner. Bridget killed Regan McGonigle. And Christine. And Karen. They all knew who she was from Southie. And now she's going to kill me, too. On the first day here Christine obviously recognized her. And then she was dead.

"Let's throw her over the cliff," Amador says, grinding a cigarette butt out with his heel at the cave entrance.

"Pick that up," Bridget says.

It would be handy if the guard was here, I think. Oh yeah, he probably went home for dinner.

"Take her into the cave. We do this the right way, with the dagger," Bridget says. "Or it's just murder."

Amador puts me down on the cave floor, not very gently I might say, then he and Hector start yammering excitedly in Spanish. My right hand is twitching slightly. The anesthesia is wearing off.

They've all put on head lamps and I can see that Bridget is running her hands over the cave wall like Dick did until suddenly one of the stones moves and she reaches behind it and grabs something. It's the bejeweled dagger.

Didn't Dick take it with him? Did he put it *back?*

"Mrrrrrpppppphhhh," I say.

"Shut up!" Hector hisses at me.

The three of them are arguing over the dagger. I close my eyes and reach in my robe pocket to twist open the plastic bag of doggie yum yums. Goliath is by my side in an instant, whining. I pull one out and he eagerly eats it. Then another. But then I feel another tongue licking my hand. I force an eye open. Devil Dog! Layla never had Devil Dog! He was waiting here for me to come back for him! Smart doggie!

Bridget hands Hector the dagger and he's coming at me, but Devil Dog bites his ankle.

"*Chingate!*" he screams, trying to shake Devil Dog off his leg.

"Don't hurt the dog," Bridget says.

Amador tries to wrest Devil Dog off Hector's leg and when he can't, he pulls his gun out of his shoulder holster but Goliath lunges at him and bites his arm, forcing him to drop it.

"Down, Goliath!" Bridget commands. "What's the *matter* with you?"

Devil Dog growls as he wrestles Hector's leg. Hector is shaking it back and forth and screaming in Spanish and he drops the dagger.

"*Bastardo!*" Hector screams. "I kill him."

The dagger is close to my hand which is trying to wake up. If I only had the strength to grab it and plunge it somewhere helpful. I wriggle my hand then flex it open and closed. And I grab the dagger just when two men dressed in black including face masks and holding what look like magnum pistols come in.

Chapter 29

The Enemy of My Friend is My Enemy or My Enemy's Friend...or Something Like That

I slip the dagger under my hip.

"It's so nice to see everyone all together," one of the orangutans—no offense meant to orangutans—says gruffly as he pats Bridget down and takes a gun out of the back of her jeans. In the darkness they don't see Amador's gun which has fallen almost within my reach. "This makes things easier."

One of the orangutans is much smaller than the other one. Amador says something to him in Spanish. It's clear he was expecting them.

"Well, well," Bridget says. I can see her face in the lamplight. She looks amused. "Smart move," she says to Amador. "Good evening, Bernardo. I thought we were going to talk. About Boston. What's the rush?"

"We don't need you for that any more, Bridget. This is just business."

The tall orangutan pushes them towards the mouth of the cave. "Take your pick," he says. "Jump or a bullet in the head."

Goliath and Devil Dog are standing tails up, unsure whose leg to bite.

I hiss at Devil Dog and he looks back at me.

"Who is that?" the tall one asks, pointing a gun loosely at me.

"She's dead," Bridget says.

"Yeah?" He comes over and kicks my leg right where the iguana slashed me, causing a searing pain to brand my brain. The anesthesia has almost worn off, but I miraculously find my *drishti* and focus, willing my body to go limp and my mouth to remain welded shut. The man loses interest in my inert form and walks back to the trio lined up at the edge of the cliff. "Who wants to go first?" he asks, pushing the point of his gun into the back of each in turn.

Focusing intently—Dick would approve, I think—I elongate my body and bend it sideways until I reach Amador's gun, pick it up, stand up and cock it.

"Drop your guns!" I yell as the men turn to me with their own guns raised.

"Pull the trigger!" Bridget yells.

Which I do, wildly without aim. I hit Hector and he crumples and tumbles off the cliff. Amador wrestles with Bernardo while Bridget starts towards me.

"I'll take that sister," she says, smiling, holding out her hand.

"No way," I say, pointing for her to go back to the cliff.

The tall orangutan comes towards me. I pull the trigger again and he winces but keeps coming. Body armor, I think. "Put it down," he commands, pointing his cannon at my head.

I take a deep breath, lay the pistol on the ground and back away a few feet, while the orangutan, never taking his eyes off me, squats down to pick it up. As soon as he touches the gun, I kick him in the face and he teeters for a minute but doesn't lose his balance.

"You stupid *gringa*!" he yells as he grabs my legs and drags me towards the cliff. Devil Dog comes running over and bites his right calf and while he instinctively bends down to touch the bite, I bring my hand holding the jewel encrusted ceremonial dagger over my head and plunge it into his shoulder, causing him to drop his gun. I kick it away from him and pick it up and put it in my robe pocket.

Amador and Bernardo are rolling on the ground and Goliath is taking bites of both of them. Suddenly a gun goes off and Amador goes limp. Bridget runs and kneels over to him. "Amador! You fool. This didn't have to happen. No!"

Goliath bites Bernardo's wrist until he lets go of his gun. I pick it up and realizing I am running out of pockets in my robe to store guns in I toss it off the cliff.

I become aware that other people are running down the ceremonial steps and I breathe a sigh of relief as I hear Dick's anxious shout, *"Huntah? Ah you heah?"*

"Dick, over here."

Devil Dog and Goliath are happily eating the doggie yum yums that I scattered over the floor.

"How did you know it was me?" Dick asks, coming close so I can see it's him in the darkness. "You never give away your position until you're sure who's who."

Mark's clone is right behind him. He's a cop. The clunky shoes! Of course, I should have seen it. "All of you, over by the cliff!" he shouts to the Zetas and Bridget.

Suddenly Mark comes down he steps. "You," he says to Bridget.

She turns around and spits at him and stomps on his foot. "I read you for a cop the minute you set foot in Casa Linda. What right do you have to come down here," she hisses.

"What right did you have to kill my wife," he says.

"One of those tarts was your wife?"

Mark glares at her.

"Oh, you mean Regan McGonigle, don't you? She was a user and a snitch. She got what was coming to her."

"You think snitch is worse than murderer?" Mark says.

"In Southie it is. I knew your wife. I *knew* her! We played hockey together. She loved my reefer. Yes, your good little cop girl, she smoked my reefer like everyone else. And she was going to snitch on me? A snitch is the lowest of the low in Southie."

Mark slaps her across the face.

Bridget slaps him back and soon they're wrestling. I want to cover my eyes. You don't want to mess with a Southie girl when her dander is up. Neither Dick nor the clone steps in to stop them and Bridget pulls a switch blade out of a sheath strapped to her ankle— she was obviously buying time before deciding who to use it on—and pops it open. Mark grabs her wrist and they struggle in some kind of weird dance, lurching towards the edge of the cliff, and in the light cast by the headlamps they look like the skeletons dancing on one of the *Dia de los Muertos* floats and I start toward them but Dick grabs my arm. "Let them finish," he says.

Mark twists the switchblade out of Bridget's grip. He waves it at her while she taunts him.

"Go ahead. Go ahead!" she laughs and she spits at him again. He slashes the blade across her chest, cutting her shirt but not breaking her skin. She steps backwards and teeters on the edge of the cliff. Mark grabs her shirt. He starts to pull her away from the edge then pauses, and for a second they look like a frozen tableau against the starry sky. Then he releases her shirt and gently touches her chest and she falls backwards into the darkness.

I close my eyes tight and let out a little whimper.

Dick collects all my guns. "This is quite an arsenal, Swanson. Do you have a permit?"

He grins at his stupid joke, but stupid jokes are one of the things I like about Dick. That and he reminds me of home. Maybe that's what I should call him: he's my *homeboy*.

"What do we do with these two?" Mark's clone asks.

"Let 'em go," Dick says, "Let's get the hell out of here."

Mark gathers me in his arms. "Swanson! When we couldn't find Hunter and Layla we got here as fast as we could. Hunter was playing us. They must have known the Zetas were planning this. They've both cleared out."

I remember what Death said to me in Jamaica Plain: "I will be seeing you in Tulum, Swanson, and you will be seeing *me*." I killed Hector. I killed a man. I could pretend it was an accident. I wasn't aiming at him, but the truth is I had a gun, I fired it and I killed a man before he could kill me. Death doesn't make distinctions like good guys and bad guys.

Then Mark whispers something delightful in my ear. And I know now what Dick meant about hearing a Southie accent in the jungle. Even amidst all this carnage, it feels like home.

Chapter 30

If It Walks Like a Duck and Talks Like a Duck....

Julie Griswold and the other Grace, whose name is Kaitlin, come to stay at Casa Linda the next morning. Dick makes a pot of coffee while Mark shoos away all the yogins and yoginis who are arriving for morning Sun Salutations. We can hear gears grinding, clutches scraping and rubber peeling as they zoom off in search of another Sun Salutation. It shouldn't be hard. This is Mexico.

"Christine recognized Bridget as soon as she got out of the Escalade," Julie says. "They went to school together."

"We saw them talking. They had their arms around each other then they disappeared," Kaitlin says. "And the next thing we know, Christine is falling off the cliff."

I groan. I mean, what was Bridget thinking? How could she not know that eventually Hunter would bring someone from Southie to a Tulum retreat? She was Southie to the bone. Maybe too Southie. I'll bet she never said Namaste even once in her whole life.

"Did you see Christine fall?" I ask.

"No. I just saw her body on the rocks. Like everyone else." She starts to cry and Julie starts to cry then so do I. Finally, someone is crying for Christine. It seems important to me that someone cry for Christine.

"And Karen? Do you know how she got lured to the cave?" I ask.

"All I know is that she was going to a midnight spirituality workshop that Layla was giving. I told her not to go. I told her the Mayans must have put a spell on that place before they died out that no one but them could ever break."

The weirdest thing in this whole tale is that the DNA results came back to Dick on his smartphone this morning and besides what Dick expected, that is, Christine's and Karen's, Bridget's and Amador's, Layla's and Hunter's DNA being all over everything, there was residual DNA in the scrapings that was a thousand years old and you'll never guess what. Layla's was a close match to it. The kind of close that archeologists use to trace descendants. So maybe she wasn't as crazy as I thought. Maybe Janab Pakal or Lord Kisin or Ah Cun Can aren't just voices in her head.

I walked down to Hunter's casa on the beach earlier this morning and it was cleared out. Dick and Mark rode down through the jungle to Layla's house but a guard wouldn't let them past the cenote. He said she was gone and that the house had new owners.

Julie and Kaitlin hold each other and cry. Me and Devil Dog join in. Senseless death. Is there any other kind?

I'm not off the hook either. I will carry Hector's death around with me till I die. Even though he was a rotter. Even though I wasn't aiming at him. I flash on the first day I was in Tulum. When I was talking to Hunter at the ruins and saw him turn into a hawk with a body in its claws. I thought I was seeing the murderer. I see now that I was seeing myself. What I've been up till now and will never be again.

"I think that's about it," Mark says. He's closed the gate on the last of the yogis and he sits down with us at the table on the hacienda veranda and pours himself a cup of coffee.

"We have some unfinished business," I tell him.

"I know."

"When does the shuttle leave for the airport?" Julie asks.

"Ten o'clock," Dick says.

Of all the horrible things which have happened on this yoga retreat, an unpleasant event was still in my future: telling the woman at the Avis counter that her car was torched and we didn't have all the insurance. And I don't have Layla anymore to get me out of the slammer.

"I want to get in a quickie," Dick says. "Anyone in?"

"Us!" Kaitlin raises her hand and the three of them go up to the yoga studio in the back building, leaving me alone with Mark.

"Do you want to know how much I knew?" he asks.

"No. I want to know which parts you didn't know. It'll probably be a shorter conversation."

"I didn't want you to get hurt. If I told you we were on to Bridget, you would have started nosing around."

"Nosing around! What do you think I am? A bloodhound?"

"You have a healthy young woman's curiosity. You're not just a pretty face, obviously. There's a whole lot going on in there."

"You could have told me what you were doing here. Jeez! I spilled my guts to you because we had something in common—losing people we loved. I've never told anyone else about how Guy and Hidalgo died. About what it did to me. About what it feels like. And I feel like you tricked it out of me. I feel like a jerk." Tears start to flow. "Did you and Dick have the whole thing planned out? Or did you just make it up off the cuff?"

"Dick was here to keep an eye on me. I've been a loose cannon since Regan died. They'll probably take me back after they put me through a battery of tests to see if I've stopped being angry. Dick's a good person, Swanson."

"So you came here to kill Bridget? Is that what you came here to do?"

"Believe it or not, I didn't know what would happen when I confronted her. I knew it had to be her, but like Dick says you have to catch someone red-handed to know for sure. You know what the worst part is? I can see my life without Regan now. Before I met you I didn't think it was possible to go on living without her. Was it so bad to talk about Guy and Hidalgo? Maybe you needed to get it out."

"Maybe I did.   But it feels like a confession under false pretenses. How can I ever trust you again?"

"I'd like you to give me a chance to make it up to you," Mark says. "Honest to god, Swanson, I never thought I'd find another woman who was my match. You were magnificent at the cave! The way you took on those thugs while you were drugged... and with no clothes on..."

"Okay, okay."

It occurs to me that one thing we definitely have in common is that last night we killed people. We didn't intend to, maybe. And maybe we didn't start the fight, but it would always be a black bond between us.

"I couldn't have done it without these two," I say. I pet Devil Dog and Goliath who are sitting at my feet. I have to take Goliath home with me. With Bridget gone he has no one to take care of him.

He helped save my life, it's the least I can do. But what am I going to do with two dogs? At least Devil Dog is compact and fits under an airplane seat. Goliath will have to be crated. And how can I take two dogs with me around Boston. I am becoming the eccentric bachelorette my uncles were always afraid I would become. Oh, look! There's that weirdo divorce lawyer with the two dogs!

"But you set me up with Bridget! You knew what would happen. That was the real plan, wasn't it? Romantic evening with Hunter indeed."

"We knew Hunter was stalling for time. Anyway, you wouldn't have been such good bait if you knew what was happening."

Mark takes my hand. "Swanson? Can you give me another chance? We can never have a normal life after all this. I'm a cop, and cops are not normal. But you're not exactly normal either."

He's right. We're not normal.

"What about Hunter? Where is he anyway?"

"I don't know. The drug money being pumped into the yoga business? That's not why I came down here. That's not my fight."

"Let's see what happens when we get home."

"Promise?"

"Promise. Now I gotta go. I gotta shower and stuff before we leave."

I am conscious that Mark is watching me go up the stairs and that all I have on is a robe, which I let hang open, enjoying my power.

Chapter 31

What Happens in Tulum, Stays in Tulum

Savas Hanna studio on Arlington Street is dark. It's the first free night I have since returning from Tulum a month ago. I had a court case downtown this afternoon and thought I would take the T from Brookline to Boston, then see if I could slip in a yoga session afterwards. I shield my eyes with my hand to see in. A sign in the foyer says, "Coming Soon: Pilates for the Masses."

As I turn away, another yogini with a mat on her shoulder goes up to the window and pounds the glass after she reads the sign. Breathe in! Then breathe out! I want to tell her.

"Too bad," she says to me. "There's a new place that just opened on Exeter St. I heard about it yesterday."

"Great," I say. "Have fun."

"You want to come?"

"Not tonight."

She adjusts her backpack and mat, runs to the T Stop and disappears down the stairs.

Snow is coming down pretty steadily. It's an early winter and all the reports say it's going to be a long one. Bad weather hysteria has set in with people stockpiling candles, batteries, tuna fish and bottled water and I've avoided grocery shopping for that reason. I just don't feel like being around crowds anymore. The feeling of something about to happen is palpable, I've had it for days, and I don't think it's a bad thing I'm waiting for. I think it's something good. But even if something wonderful happens, I want to be able to enjoy it by myself before I share it with anyone. It's probably all the yoga I've been doing. Ever since Tulum, I've been sneaking in short practices in my apartment whenever I have fifteen minutes and I've been enjoying the solitude which no longer feels like loneliness.

I've put off seeing Mark although he calls me almost every day, at first pleading with me to see him, then finally just leaving messages that are corny jokes.

"Why are math books so sad?" he says in one message, "Because they have so many problems!" Beat. Beat. "Call me!"

Corny jokes are the way to my funny bone, no question about it. And I like Mark. He's a guy my uncles would treat like a son. What does it mean that I can wait to see him?

I decide to walk home to Brookline, which is a long hike, but since I stopped wearing my Jimmy Choos everywhere my calf muscles have elongated and I find I actually *enjoy* walking. I walk down Newbury Street which is lined with all the chic shops. Hermés, Chanel, Marc Jacobs, the Nielsen Gallery which is showing my favorite artist, Vincent Sferrazza, whose work Dick introduced me to a year ago. We went to a gallery opening and he said I was an odalisque and he wanted to paint me and I almost knocked people over running out of there. Not only was I scared of sitting nude for an artist, I thought he might be able to see into my soul. It's Thursday night and I can see the opening party through the giant bay window. Plastic tumblers full of wine. Women in little black dresses. A vase of Siberian irises on a table in the window. I stare at the party through the glass and I see Vincent Sferrazza looking back at me. He raises his plastic glass to me and smiles. I smile back, wave and move on.

Tiny white lights are wrapped around the trees which line the street and the stores already have Christmas decorations in their windows. I stop to look at the shoes in the window of John Fleuvog. Definitely cool, but for the absolute first time in my life, I have no desire to rush in and buy—even the very cool cobalt blue suede zippered booties with wedge heels. My soul is expanding at the expense of my soles. I laugh at myself and walk away.

My phone vibrates and I look to see who it is: Uncle Joe. I touch the ignore button and put it back in my purse. I know something is going to happen and I don't want Uncle Joe and Uncle Stevie—as much as I love them—to try to steer me in the right direction.

When I reach Exeter Street, I decide to turn. I should check out the place for future reference. I definitely need a place to practice seeing how my last guru is AWOL. I see light coming from a second story and by the fogged windows I know it's a yoga studio. I open the door to the foyer and look down the names on the buzzers, finally resting on "Namas Day."

I throw back my head and laugh and my heart beats fast as I run up the stairs. The class is already in session, but the woman at the desk takes my sixteen dollars and makes me sign a release. Then I shove another ten dollars at her and grab a water. I change hurriedly and step into the back of the class. I snap open my ridiculous yellow mat and go into down dog with the rest of the class.

A familiar male voice is commanding the class. "Death is part of life. If you don't accept that, you can never be at peace."

I wait expectantly until finally a pair of male hands adjusts my hips and says, "You're going to leave here more peaceful than you've ever felt. I feel the need in you and I'm going to make sure it happens. Serenity is my business."